MOUNT PROSPECT
PUBLIC LIBRARY

David Hill

SEE YA, SIMON

D0101291

PUFFIN BOOKS

PUFFIN BOOKS
Published by the Penguin Group
Penguin Books USA Inc., 375 Hudson Street, New York, New York 10014, U.S.A.
Penguin Books Ltd, 27 Wrights Lane, London W8 5TZ, England
Penguin Books Australia Ltd, Ringwood, Victoria, Australia
Penguin Books Canada Ltd, 10 Alcorn Avenue, Toronto, Ontario, Canada M4V 3B2
Penguin Books (N.Z.) Ltd, 182–190 Wairau Road, Auckland 10, New Zealand

Penguin Books Ltd, Registered Offices: Harmondsworth, Middlesex, England

Originally published in New Zealand by Mallinson Rendel Publishers Ltd.,
New Zealand, 1992.
First published in the United States of America by Dutton Children's Books,
a division of Penguin Books USA Inc., 1994
Published in Puffin Books, 1996

1 3 5 7 9 10 8 6 4 2

Copyright © David Hill, 1992
All rights reserved

THE LIBRARY OF CONGRESS HAS CATALOGED THE DUTTON EDITION AS FOLLOWS:
Hill, David.
See ya, Simon / by David Hill.—1st American ed.
p. cm.
Summary: Over the years, fourteen–year–old Nathan has learned a lot about
muscular dystrophy from his best friend but is unprepared for Simon's
rapid decline and approaching death.
ISBN 0-525-45247-8
[1. Muscular dystrophy—Fiction. 2. Physically handicapped— Fiction.
3. Friendship—Fiction. 4. Death—Fiction.] I. Title. II. Title: See you, Simon.
PZ7.H5489Se 1994 [Fic]—dc20 93-39870 CIP AC

Puffin Books ISBN 0-14-037056-0

Printed in the United States of America

Except in the United States of America, this book is sold subject to the condition that
it shall not, by way of trade or otherwise, be lent, re–sold, hired out, or otherwise
circulated without the publisher's prior consent in any form of binding or cover
other than that in which it is published and without a similar condition
including this condition being imposed on the subsequent purchaser.

OTHER PUFFIN BOOKS YOU MAY ENJOY

We lined up at t   4 .

servants," Sim

   I pulled on the wheelchair. Todd and Haare pushed. Jason pushed Todd and Haare....We heaved. We hauled. The chair stayed put.

   We tried again. The chair struggled up the damp grassy bank about two meters, then slowly slid back down again. "I could grow old right here," said Simon.

   "Maybe if you four get in the chair and I do the pushing?" suggested Simon. We ignored him and strained with all our strength. The chair skidded round in a half circle and ended up facing away from the bank.

   There was a noise behind us like corrugated iron sliding down a pile of bricks, and I recognized Alex Wilson's laugh. "You guys want to put more sugar on your cereal!" he sneered. "Let a real man have a go!"

   The real man waved the rest of us aside and got in behind the chair. He held the back supports with both hands and lunged forward. Movement! No, not the chair—Alex. His feet slipped backward about half a meter.

   My stare met Simon's eyes. One of them slowly closed and opened in a wink, then flickered downward toward the controls of his wheelchair. My own eyes moved in the same direction, and I produced a snort which I quickly changed to a cough. Simon had both wheelchair brakes on! No wonder we hadn't been able to move the little fink!

AN NCSS–CBC "NOTABLE CHILDREN'S TRADE BOOK IN THE FIELD OF SOCIAL STUDIES"

MOUNT PROSPECT
PUBLIC LIBRARY

In Memory of N.J.B., 1975–1990

CHAPTER
One

Simon scored this amazing goal in soccer today.

Mr. Johnston said we could have a game, even though it was still really the summer sports season. He got us all to line up in alphabetical order, boys and girls mixed. There were a lot of arguments over whether Todd Martin came before or after Melissa McDonald, and of course Alex Wilson went and put himself under A instead of W. Then Mr. Johnston came along, saying "Eeny-meeny, miney-mo, eeny-meeny, miney-mo," till he'd divided the class into two teams—the Eeny-meenys and the Miney-mos.

Nelita Travers told him he'd forgotten the referee and the linesmen, but Mr. Johnston said it was okay, he'd be all three. "You haven't got six arms and six legs," said Nelita, who works through jokes like our dog works through a plate of hamburger.

Mr. Johnston was ready for her. "Maybe not," he said. "But since I'm a teacher, I've got eyes in the back of my head. That'll do instead." Nelita went off to join the Miney-mos, calling, "Friends, Romans, phys ed teachers, lend me your eyes!" I went off to guard Brady West. So did three other guys.

Simon was goalie for our team, the Eeny-meenys. For the first part of the game, the ball was down in the other half, and he didn't have anything to do. He just kept zooming backward and forward between the goalposts, yelling out, "Too chicken to come near me, eh?" and "Here we go! Here we go!" like the fans at English soccer games do.

Then someone gave the ball an almighty boot, and it went flying way upfield where Simon was waiting, all by himself. "Look out, Simon! Hey, Superstopper! Catch it, Simon!" we Eeny-meenys were yelling.

Simon didn't have to catch it. The ball bounced, and bounced again, and bounced a third time, and landed smack in his lap. "Who's a well-trained little soccer ball, then?" he said.

Everyone was yelling for Simon to chuck them the ball. But he didn't. Instead, he put the ball down between his feet, pulled his wheelchair throttle open, and started motoring straight downfield toward the other goal.

Nelita was the nearest player from the Miney-mo team. She stood with her mouth hanging open while Simon and his wheelchair came straight at her. At the last moment, she jumped out of the way. One of the arms on the chair jabbed her in the backside as Simon trundled past. Nelita stood there rubbing her bum and shouting, "Hit-and-run driver! Road hog!"

By this time, half our Eeny-meeny team was trotting along beside Simon, calling for the ball. "Simon! Simon! Chuck it here, Simon!" We must have looked like a lunch line chasing after Meals-On-Wheels.

Simon didn't take any notice. "Get stuffed!" he replied. There was a huge grin on his face.

Haare Haunui was goalie for the Miney-mos. As Simon got nearer and nearer, Haare dropped on his knees and pretended to pray. Then he scrambled across and tried to hide behind one of his own goalposts.

Simon drove his wheelchair straight between the posts and into the back of the net. "Goal!" all us Eeny-meenys yelled.

The Miney-mos started arguing. "It can't be a goal!" Todd Martin shouted.

"Why not?" Simon wanted to know. "The ball went over the line, didn't it?"

"Yeah, but—," Todd tried to say.

"I had it between my feet, didn't I?" Simon interrupted him.

"Yeah, but—"

"Then it was a goal, wasn't it?"

Todd tried to say something else, but everyone was clapping and cheering too loudly to hear him. Mr. Johnston's face had turned traffic-light red from laughing, and he'd started hiccuping. He managed to get enough breath to give a feeble toot on his whistle.

"One, nil," he gurgled. "Back to halfway, everyone. Simon, you can reverse-thrust back to your own goal now."

"Sorry, Mr. Johnston," said Simon, who didn't look at all sorry. "Someone'll have to give me a hand. I've got the soccer net caught in one wheel, and I think my battery's gone flat."

Oh hell, I groaned to myself. Now I'll have to push Simon home after school. And that new wheelchair of his is *heavy*.

Simon got his new chair at the start of the year. Last year he'd had a lighter one that he pushed with his hands, but over the summer holidays his muscles had gotten a lot weaker. By the time we came back this year, he didn't have much strength left in his shoulders and his upper arms. Now he's got this flash chair with a battery-driven, two-horsepower motor. "News flash, Nathan!" he said when he rang me up in the holidays to tell me about it. "They're sending me to the electric chair!"

The new chair can usually go for two or three days at a slow speed before its battery needs recharging, but when Simon hoons around in it the way he did at soccer today, it runs out much faster.

The first week after he got it, he burned up and down to the shops about a thousand times a day, trying it out on the sidewalks and the ramp up to the town library. So of course, on the first day back at school, the battery ran out in the middle of the main road.

The only place Simon can cross the main road is at the pedestrian crossing, where they've got concrete ramps sloping down from the sidewalk. Simon reckons it's time they designed a bungee-jumping wheelchair so that people can drive off the edge of the sidewalk anywhere they want to and go crashing down into the gutter.

Anyway, the first day of school I'd met him at the dairy as usual. He'd been in and bought a take-away milk shake. "Hey, Nathan! Beware of drinking drivers!" he called when he saw me coming. He couldn't drink anything like that in his old chair because he needed both hands to push the wheels.

We started off down the ramp and onto the crossing. Traffic always stops for Simon—he never has to wait while cars keep tearing past. Sometimes he'll give the drivers a wave and a bow, and say, "Thank you, my loyal subjects." He's an expert at being embarrassing.

On this day, his big flash new chair whirred out into the middle of the crossing—and stopped. Just like that. It was the first time the battery had run out, and neither Simon nor I knew what was happening. He kept pulling at the throttle, but the motor just made whining noises, like our dog when it's bolted down its breakfast too fast and is feeling sick.

By this time there were about six trucks and ten cars lined up waiting at the crossing. Since it was a kid in a wheelchair, they didn't like to honk. "Chicken!" Simon finally yelled at them. "Push, slave!" he said to me. He got to school that day by one man power, not two horsepower.

Even when he had to get the new chair, I didn't realize how much worse Simon had gotten. But then about a month after term started, they took our class photos.

I looked like a total idiot, of course. I always do. I hate smiling for the camera, and I'm always glaring as if someone's just taken away all my Rusty Guts tapes. Alex Wilson looked like a half-trained orangutan, which is about right. Brady West looked—how many words are there that rhyme with *fantastic*?

Mum was with Mrs. Kuklinski from next door when I got home, so I showed them both the prison portrait. It was a real shock when Mrs. Kuklinski said, "Poor Simon Shaw. He's gone downhill, hasn't he?"

Later on, when I put the photo next to last year's, I could see what Mrs. Kuklinski meant. You don't notice the changes when you see someone nearly every day, but in last year's photo Simon was sitting quite straight in his chair, his face was rounder, and his arms looked thicker and stronger. In this year's photo he's bent forward, and his face and body are both skinnier. He looks sort of fragile. He's not growing up like the rest of us. He's growing down.

Then, only about two days after the photo, something happened in English that brought it home even more.

Ms. Kidman had been reading us this poem about old age. "Grow old along with me. / The best is yet to be." Actually, there's a fair number in our class I don't particularly want to grow old along with. Being fourteen along with them is bad enough.

Then we got to talking about getting old. "Remember, being old does *not* mean being over thirty-five!" Ms. Kidman warned us. "So mind your language."

"How do you know when you *are* old, anyway?" someone asked.

"When your birthday candles cost more than your cake," said Nelita. At least it was better than most of her jokes.

Just about everyone in the class agreed they were a bit scared of getting old. They didn't like to think about not being able to do things any longer, or not being able to look after themselves and losing their dignity. Things like that. Ms. Kidman kept saying that old age didn't *have* to be that way, but everyone was getting pretty depressed about the whole idea.

"Well," said Ms. Kidman at last, "is there anyone in the class who's *not* worried about getting old?"

Simon's hand went up. "I'm not," he said.

"Good, Simon," exclaimed Ms. Kidman in relief. "Why's that?" And suddenly I saw her try to stop herself as she realized what was coming.

"Well, I'm not going to get to old age, am I?" replied Simon. "I'm going to be dead first."

There was absolute silence in the classroom. Nobody knew what to say. Nobody knew where to look. I felt really angry at Simon. He doesn't need to say these things. We hadn't been trying to leave him out or anything.

He must have realized he'd upset people, because he gave

an embarrassed sort of grin. "Tell you what. When you lot do get old, you can send me a postcard and tell me what it's like. Send it airmail."

Ms. Kidman is really quick, and she picked this one up like a flash. "Good idea, Simon, but they'll have to learn a bit of punctuation first. Which reminds me—take out your folders, please, people."

There was the usual moaning and groaning, but you could tell that everyone was pleased to escape. Soon they were working away busily, Simon with them.

But I couldn't get what he'd just said out of my mind. After all, it's true. Simon's my best friend, and sometime in the next year or two, he's going to die.

CHAPTER
TWO

I thought about Simon this morning before school when I was walking the dog. My little sister, Fiona the Moaner, is supposed to walk him on Thursday mornings, but she always manages to get out of it somehow.

This morning I'd told her that if she sneaked into my room and mucked about with my role-playing books one more time, I'd break every bone in her body, starting with her big toes. She went rushing off to tell Mum, squealing, "Mum! Mum! Nathan's going to beat me up!" Then Mum said she wasn't having any male violence flaunted in *her* house, so I could walk the dog and think about behaving like a civilized human being.

How you're supposed to be civilized in a house that has Fiona the Moaner in it, I don't know. She stuck her tongue out at me when Mum wasn't looking. Next time I'll threaten to break her tongue first.

The dog was hauling me along the sidewalk, looking for trees and shrubs to piddle against. Our dog has no concern for the environment. Sooner or later he's going to kill every green living thing in the street. Serve him right when it happens. Maybe then he'll run out of ways to embarrass me.

Our dog is a big one, a cross between a Labrador and a brontosaurus. He's like a brontosaurus in other ways, too. I reckon his brain is the size of a pea.

I shouldn't really have said I was walking the dog. He walks me. I just lean back and sidewalk-ski along after him. I'm hoping that one day he'll take off when Fiona's in charge of him, and they'll both vanish over the horizon and never be seen again. Simon reckons I should fit a towrope to the dog and attach him to the wheelchair. He says it'd save him having to get a battery-charge so often.

Simon has muscular dystrophy. It's a disease where the muscles of your body slowly get weaker and just waste away.

It usually starts when you're about three or four. Your hips get stiff and it's hard to walk. Kids with muscular dystrophy start falling a lot, and because their legs are getting weaker, they can only stand up again by pushing and pulling themselves up with their arms.

After a while you need sticks or crutches to walk with. By the time you're ten or twelve you're usually in a wheelchair. Then the muscles in your shoulders and arms start to fail as well.

There's no cure for muscular dystrophy, though Simon takes antibiotic drugs and does physical therapy exercises to try and keep his muscles working for a bit longer. If you have MD, you usually die in your teens.

You can't catch muscular dystrophy from germs. It's passed on to you from your parents, even though they don't have it themselves. You get it from certain genes.

Simon makes sick jokes about it. He says that's why he never wears jeans, though in fact he can't wear them because they're too tight and awkward for him to get on. Only about one person in five thousand gets MD, and only boys get the worst sort, which is what Simon has.

I didn't know Simon much before high school. We went to play center together, though I don't remember it—I didn't keep many notes during my four-year-old days. Then Simon went to the Catholic primary school. I used to see this little guy on crutches and then in a wheelchair downtown, but I didn't really take much notice of him. Sometimes he wouldn't be around for a while—he spent a lot of time in hospital when they were running tests on him.

I remember one thing that happened before we met up at high school, though. Some stupid fool started a rumor that Simon had AIDS, and that's why he was sick.

Next thing you know, some parents wouldn't let their kids play with Simon, in case they caught something from him. One father even rang up the Catholic school and said he didn't want his child sitting next to Simon in class.

Then one afternoon a mother who'd come to pick her kid up after school found her talking to Simon while he waited for his mum to come in the van and get him. This other mother started calling to her kid things like, "Come away. Quickly! You know you're not supposed to go near that boy!" When Mrs. Shaw arrived in the van and saw this woman yelling, and Simon sitting there all white-faced, she went totally apeshit.

So, even though he wasn't at our primary school, our principal got up in assembly one morning and told us a bit about what Simon's muscular dystrophy was, and how these other rumors about him were just ignorant rubbish.

After that, I'd usually say "G'day" to Simon if I passed him down at the shops. You often do that in a small town like ours, anyway. Sometimes I'd say, "How's it going?" and if he was in his wheelchair he'd usually say, "With a rubber band," or "About one mile per hour." So we sort of knew each other by the time we got to high school, and when we ended up in the same class, we soon became friends.

It's easy to forget that Simon's not going to live on like the rest of us. A few muscular dystrophy patients get mentally affected, but Simon's so quick, and he's got such a wicked sense of humor, that once you know him you hardly notice he's in a wheelchair—till something reminds you.

It was like that a few weeks after this year started, when they had a back-to-school dance.

Dances are pretty tame affairs at our school. Todd Martin says that at the school he went to last year, kids at their dances kept rushing to turn the lights off all the time. Then the teachers had to go around prying couples apart with a crowbar. I think Todd may have been exaggerating just a bit—crowbars can leave nasty bruises.

There was one time at last year's end-of-school dance, when Alex Wilson's big brother and his girlfriend started kissing in the middle of the floor. They had their eyes closed as if they were being carried away by passion or something. I personally reckon the only thing that's likely to carry away anyone in Alex Wilson's family is men in white coats.

When Mr. Johnston saw them, he went up and squeezed their noses between his thumbs and fingers. Since their mouths were jammed together, they had to let each other go in order to breathe. When they saw Mr. Johnston grinning at them, they looked pretty silly.

I agree with what Mr. Johnston did—there's a time and a place for everything. My time and place would be . . . I'll tell you when I find one.

There were hordes of kids from every year at our back-to-school dance—third formers (turds), us fourth formers (stale turds), fifth and sixth and seventh formers (moldy/dried/fossilized turds). A lot of people turned up dressed in black to show they were in mourning for having to go back to school.

Simon arrived about half an hour after the dance started. Mr. Shaw brought him in their van. It's got a power hoist that lifts Simon and his wheelchair in and out of the back. When he's in the van, he sometimes drives up and down inside, deliberately banging his chair into the walls and yelling, "Let me out! Let me out! My parents are trying to sell me to a beauty contest!"

He rolled into the assembly hall. There was a really loud tape just finishing, with sounds of a crowd cheering and whistling, so Simon came in waving his hands and saying, "Thank you, fans! Thank you!"

He parked his chair beside one of the rows of seats they had around the hall, and we watched the girls for a while.

"Becky Klenner's jeans look tighter than they did last dance," Simon said.

"Yeah," I agreed. "So does Brady West's sweater." By a coincidence I happened to have spent most of the last half hour watching Brady.

"You're right," grinned Simon. "I'll just check my pulse. I could be getting overexcited."

Then, just as the music started for the next number, Becky and Nelita Travers and Lana Patu suddenly came tearing over to us. They're all really neat-looking girls, and I hardly knew which one of them to stare at first.

"Hey, Simon, come on!" said Becky. "Do you want to boogie?"

"Yeah, Simon," Lana said. "Come and have a whirl."

"Nathan!" yelped Simon, pretending to be scared. "Nathan! Save me!"

But the girls already had him. Becky was pushing the wheelchair and Nelita and Lana were holding his hands— lucky guy! They were whirling him in big circles across the floor, swooping him in and out among the other kids, and yelling, "Look out! It's *Dirty Dancing!*"

The others were cheering and whistling. Simon was laughing and calling, *"Don't* save me! *Don't* save me!" His face was pink and his eyes were shiny.

Then I saw Ms. Kidman. She was standing in the doorway to the kitchen, where the teachers go to try to escape for a few minutes. She must have come out to see what all the noise was about.

She looked surprised, as if she couldn't quite believe what she was seeing. Then she smiled like all the others. But instead of starting to laugh, she started to cry. She stood there smiling and crying without making a sound.

I knew what she was thinking, as clearly as if she'd written it up on the board in English and told us to copy it down. By the time next year's back-to-school dance came, Simon would be . . . where? I stared at where he was still being whirled around in the middle of the floor. Melissa McDonald and Brady West were holding his hands now. Hell, I felt jealous!

When I looked back at the kitchen doorway, Ms. Kidman was gone.

Actually, the girls and Simon were all breaking a school rule, pushing his chair around the hall like that. He's not supposed to be in places where his tires leave black marks on the floor.

The week before the dance he'd gotten into trouble for doing wheelies in the corridors. If he keeps the brake on for one wheel and pulls the throttle suddenly, his chair skids round in a circle. By the time he'd shown Todd, Haare, Jason Webster, and me this about three times, the floor looked as if an entire Sunday school of Hell's Angels had burned through the corridor. That's what Mr. Packman, our science teacher, said when he was telling Simon off, anyway, and it seemed like a pretty good comparison to me.

Simon gets away with murder sometimes. And the crafty sod knows exactly how to play on people's sympathy.

This year we've got Mr. Antill for math again. We had him last year in the third form, too. Everyone calls him "Antilla the Hun" because he's so strict. They don't call him that to his face, mind you. They call him sir, spelled *c-u-r*, Simon reckons.

One time in the third form, Simon hadn't done his math homework. He told me on the way to school that he hadn't even looked at it. He'd spent the evening watching a movie on TV, *The Lord of the Rings*, which was the role-playing game we were all into last year. I was a bit hacked off with him. I'd wanted to watch the movie, too, but it had taken me nearly two hours to do the assignment.

So when Antilla the Hun asked Simon a question almost straight away, I couldn't help feeling it served him right.

"How did you solve the first problem, Simon?" Antilla growled.

Simon didn't even blink. "I couldn't do my math last night, Mr. Antill," he said.

The rest of our class held their breath, except for Nelita, who gave a little squeak. Antilla's bottom jaw started to clench tight and his eyes started to turn red. "And—why

—not?" he rumbled, sounding like an avalanche picking up speed.

Simon gave a vague wave at his wheelchair and his useless legs. "I'm afraid I was . . . I just . . . I couldn't . . ." He let his voice trail away.

Antilla the Hun's jaw went sort of slack, and his eyes went back to their normal pink color. He even gave a sympathetic nod. "Ah yes, of course, never mind. Well, Becky, you tell us your answer."

Simon managed to keep a perfectly straight face for about twenty seconds, till Antilla had begun tearing strips off Haare. Then he looked across the aisle at me and gave me a huge wink. You cunning sod! I thought to myself, and shook my fist at him.

I should have known better. Antilla the Hun swung around. "Did I see your hand go up, Nathan? Are you going to show us that you have slightly more intelligence than your friend Haare?"

"Ah . . . er . . . no, Mr. Hu—Mr. Antill," I managed to stammer. "I was just going to say I couldn't do that one about the sets, either."

"Really?" said Antilla, with a smile like a shark that's seen its morning meal approaching. "I suppose you spent all last evening watching television, did you?"

And to make it worse, Simon put on a sad look, shook his head at me, and said so that people near us could hear, "Really! Nathan!"

CHAPTER

Three

I'd never hold anything like that homework business against Simon, though. It would be so easy to spend all your time feeling sorry for yourself if you were him, and he hardly ever does that.

More often he gets ratty because people at school are too soft on him. If Ms. Kidman reads a story he's written aloud in class, and the other kids tell him, "Good one, Simon," he reckons they're saying it because of him and not because of the story. When Mr. Rata wrote on his social studies assignment, *Well researched, well presented, well organized, well written, well done! 18/20,* Simon went around muttering that if he'd been anyone else, he'd have only gotten eleven out of twenty.

"I don't like people smarming over me if I haven't deserved

it," he told me. "It makes me feel like . . . like there's something wrong with me." And he gave me one of his looks that dare you to say something.

At other times, he comes out with things that make you want to swallow as hard as you can. "Nathan?" he said one morning, when he was rolling and I was walking to school, while the other kids biked past us, calling out and laughing to one another. "Nathan, what's it feel like to ride a bike?"

Another time he got me to tell him everything I could see over people's front fences as we were going along. In his wheelchair he only comes up to my chest.

It was pretty funny, actually. I gave him a sort of tour-bus commentary as we went past each place. "Now we pass the unmown beauty of number sixty-three, where Cuddles the rottweiler has left piles of dog crap in every corner." Some of the people who were out in their yards didn't look too pleased, though.

Then there was the Saturday afternoon when Todd, Haare, Jason, and I were around at Simon's for our usual role-playing game.

We've had a sort of unofficial group going for nearly a year now. We play games like Dungeons and Dragons. There are instruction books with a story to work through, usually a science fiction or a fantasy one. You choose characters, and then you roll the ten-sided or sixteen-sided or twenty-four-sided dice and argue like hell over what's supposed to happen to you.

Actually, Jason's not always at our games. He more often than not manages to injure himself before he even gets there.

Once he fell off his bike coming out of his gate, and he had a close encounter of the painful kind with the hedge.

Anyway, the game we were playing that particular Saturday was Space Master, and one part of it was about having to dream your way out of a Werespell that the Balrogs had put you under.

We all had some pretty lurid ideas for dreams that I'd better not mention here, though it was interesting how many times Brady West came up in them.

Then Simon said right out of the blue, "When I have dreams, I can walk and run in them. A lot of it's slow-motion running, you know, like you have in dreams. But even that's pretty good for me."

He didn't say anything else for a bit. Then he gave a shrug and said, "I guess my dreams haven't caught up to me yet."

It's Saturday today, and I was going round to Simon's again this afternoon for role-playing with the other guys. I had to walk the dog first, and watch him water blast a few more shrubs to a lingering death. Fiona the Moaner dried the dishes for me while I was out. There's a faint chance she may grow up into a normal person after all. Then she gave me a drawing she'd done for Simon.

"What's it meant to be?" I asked. "An escaped sofa chasing a pack of spiders?"

Fiona the Moaner got nasty. "It's Simon and his wheelchair in your room at school!" she shouted. "Haven't you got eyes?"

I felt like telling her that I wouldn't have eyes for much

longer if I had to look at her drawings, but I thought I'd better not. Mum hasn't been in a very good mood for the last few days. She got a letter from Dad on Wednesday saying he was sorry to hear she was having financial problems, but he'd spent more money than he could afford in the last two months, and wasn't it time she sold some of the household luxuries she was still clinging to?

"Household luxuries!" Mum snarled. "I wonder if he means the washing machine that won't spin properly, or the vacuum cleaner that won't suck properly?" I guess Dad must have gotten another expensive girlfriend.

I was just turning into the main road, on my way to get some snacks for role-playing, when Simon's mum and dad picked me up in their van. They were going down to the shops, too. Simon's big sister, Kirsti, was with them.

Okay, there's nearly ten years age difference between them, but when you look at Kirsti and then at Fiona the Moaner, it's hard to believe that they belong to the same human race, let alone the same sex.

Everyone says Fiona has big brown eyes and lovely fine hair. So does the dog, I tell them. "Ooh, she'll break a few hearts when she's older," they say. Personally, I feel very sorry for any poor guy who falls for my sister in about six- or seven-years' time. How'd you like to end up going out with someone who does drawings of people with four fingers and no ears?

Now Kirsti is different altogether. She's seventeen and she is really something. In fact, I reckon she looks quite a lot like Brady West. Okay, she's a bit old for my tastes, but last Christmas she gave me a hug under a piece of mistletoe the Shaws had put up in their living room, and—and I can't wait for Christmas to come around again this year!

Simon's mum and dad are neat people. They must have lots of hard times with Simon, but they don't let it show. Mum—my mum—said once that having to cope with a handicapped child was supposed to make good marriages better and bad marriages worse. "The Shaws belong to the first lot, all right," she told me. She didn't say anything, but you could tell she was wondering how Dad would have handled things if anything like that had happened to them. Maybe he would have surprised us all.

The Shaws' van has got one of those Disabled Person stickers on it, which means they can park in specially re-served places. Today they were in a hurry to get to the supermarket before it closed, so even though Simon wasn't with them, Mrs. Shaw zoomed into the parking place marked with a wheelchair.

I waited in the van while the three of them hurried into the supermarket. The car park was just about full, and there was a big gray BMW cruising up and down, trying to find a space near the door. The driver kept glaring at me and the Shaws' van as if he didn't believe there was anyone disabled at all. I was starting to feel a bit embarrassed.

Finally, the driver stopped and lowered his window. Power windows! He leaned out toward me and started to say something.

At exactly the same time, Mr. and Mrs. Shaw and Kirsti came out of the supermarket. Mr. Shaw looked at the car,

24

and straight away he put on this awful limp, dragging one leg and hanging onto the side of the supermarket trolley as if he could hardly stand. I was biting the insides of my cheeks so I wouldn't burst out laughing, and Mrs. Shaw and Kirsti were doing the same.

"Sorry to hold you up!" Mr. Shaw called out in a quavery voice to the driver. "Afraid I'm having a bad day with the old creeping gangrene!" His limp got even worse than before.

The driver hardly knew where to look. He gave a sickly grin and shot off toward the far end of the car park. The moment he'd gone, Mrs. Shaw gave Mr. Shaw a whack across the backside with her handbag. And the moment she did that, there was a horrified gasp from another driver, who'd just seen this vicious woman beating a poor helpless cripple.

Simon was at home after having his usual Saturday session with the physical therapist. He sometimes feels a bit stiff and sore afterward. Because Simon's arm and shoulder muscles are definitely getting weaker, the therapist is trying to see what things are hardest for him to do at home so he can teach Simon movements that will help him do some of these things.

Lately, Simon's been having trouble reaching out for the dice in our role-playing games, even though he could do it quite easily about a month ago. Sometimes one of us has to move the dice closer to him, so he can scoop them into the cup.

I'd brought a headline with me for Simon this afternoon.

He and I started the headline game a couple of months

back, after Ms. Kidman did a unit on newspapers with us in English. She told us that there's this old story among newspaper editors about the perfect headline, the one that makes everyone really want to rush out and buy the paper.

Apparently the perfect headline should have four things in it—religion, royalty, sex, and mystery. And Ms. Kidman said some paper once came out with the headline— HEAVENS! SAYS DUCHESS. I'M PREGNANT. WHO DONE IT?

Simon was saying on the way home one afternoon, a couple of months ago, that the *Northern News* has some headlines that are about as good, or as bad, as that.

The *Northern News* comes out once a week, and its front page nearly always has some sex and violence scandal in huge letters. Todd Martin says it should be called the *Northern Spews* because it makes you want to throw up. Simon said that if he ever swallowed an aspirin without asking his parents first, the *Northern News* would run a headline reading CRIPPLED TEENAGER IN DRUG-THEFT SENSATION.

When I was coming back from being walked by the dog first thing this afternoon, I saw the week's *Northern Spews* poster being put up outside the dairy. It was a beauty—TV STAR IN BACKYARD UNDERWEAR ROMP.

I told Mr. and Mrs. Shaw about it in the van. Mr. Shaw shook his head and pretended to be sad. "Why doesn't anything interesting like that ever happen in *our* street?" he asked.

CHAPTER
Four

Mrs. Shaw took photos of us at role-playing this afternoon. We were all sitting round the table in their living room—Todd and Haare and Jason and Simon and me—rapt in this Lair of the White Wolf game, when the flash went off.

I got a shock, and said a word that would have sent Fiona the Moaner rushing off to tell Mum if I'd been at home. Mrs. Shaw just laughed. "Sorry, Nathan, I should have asked first," she said.

The Shaws take lots of photos of Simon. "It's because I'm so gorgeous," he says. "My true beauty has to be recorded for posterity."

He's different from me about having his photo taken. Like I said, I hate smiling for the camera, and I always end up looking like one of those mug shots on the "Crimewatch" TV program. Simon doesn't mind at all, but he doesn't look at the pictures when they're developed, and he won't ever look back at photos of himself when he was smaller. He got really nasty with Kirsti one day when she joked about bringing out the album and showing us what a dear ickle bubsy-wubsy he had been.

"Poor kid. I can understand him feeling that way," said Mum when I told her.

I heard Mrs. Kuklinski talking to Mum about Simon once. Mrs. Kuklinski's friend, Mrs. Mason, used to baby-sit for the Shaws when Kirsti was little, and she still sits for Simon if he's going to be by himself for more than an hour.

Mrs. Shaw told Mrs. Mason, who told Mrs. Kuklinski, who told Mum, who didn't know that I was listening—this is how vital information usually gets spread around in our neighborhood. She said that when Simon first started having trouble walking, Mrs. Shaw felt sure it was because she used to smoke before Simon was born, even though she gave it up the moment she knew she was having him. And because their house is fairly close to one of those huge power pylons, she even wondered for a while if the electricity in the cables might have affected Simon's nervous system.

When the Shaws found out it was muscular dystrophy, they felt almost relieved, because at last they knew what they were up against.

But then Mrs. Shaw started feeling that it was her fault again. The gene that gives you muscular dystrophy can only come from your mother. Mrs. Kuklinski said that Mrs. Shaw used to cry for hours every night and say she wished she'd never been able to have children. Then this would never have happened.

Kirsti has to live with it, too. She won't get MD herself, but she might have the gene, and any baby boy she has could end up like Simon. They can carry out tests now, before a baby is born, to see if it's male or female. What are Kirsti and her partner going to do if she's expecting a boy?

Simon says that for a long time his parents wouldn't do anything that took them away from him. They wouldn't go out at night and leave him with a baby-sitter. They wouldn't even go for a walk round the block without taking him. At first, Mr. Shaw would piggyback him everywhere. Later, they'd push him in his wheelchair.

It used to bug Simon after a while. He wanted his parents to go out and do things. He reckons they have to live their own lives, not just his life with him, which I reckon is a pretty good way of putting it.

And anyway, he wanted to be by himself sometimes. Just to see what it felt like, he said. In the hospital and at home, there were always people around him. He could hardly ever be private.

He was telling me this way back in the third form. I hadn't done much thinking then about the sorts of things that Simon could do or couldn't do. So, like an idiot, I asked him, "Why don't you just go off by yourself for a bit, if you want to be private?"

The moment I said it, I could have bitten my head off. Of course, Simon sat in his wheelchair and grinned at me. "Who's a stupid geek, then?" he asked.

To go back to Mrs. Mason—remember her? She is number two in the Mrs. Shaw, Mrs. Mason, Mrs. Kuklinski, Mum, Nathan information service. Well, after a while, she got fed up. She'd offered lots of times to baby-sit for Simon, just like she had for Kirsti, but Mr. and Mrs. Shaw always had some excuse for staying home.

Finally, Mrs. Mason went over and told Simon's parents that if they didn't go out and have an evening by themselves, she was going to lie down on the sidewalk outside their house and kick and scream. So they went out and had an evening by themselves!

Now Mrs. Mason goes over to the Shaws every second Thursday, and Simon's parents have been able to see their own friends again. Simon says they enjoy the break. So does he. Mrs. Mason lets him have twice as much dessert as his mum ever does.

It's a bit weird, though. One of Mr. and Mrs. Shaw's favorite TV programs is "News Digest," and they've just shifted it from Tuesday night to Thursday night.

Mr. and Mrs. Shaw really want to stay at home and watch it, but every second Thursday Mrs. Mason arrives and kicks them out. Then she and Simon settle down in front of the television and watch "News Digest." Meanwhile, Simon's mum and dad have gone tearing round to their friends'

house. There they settle down in front of the television—
and watch "News Digest."

Simon's place is rigged up with all sorts of gadgets to help
him do things for himself.

I couldn't believe it the first time I stayed the night there.
It takes him a long time to have a shower, so he has one at
night before he goes to bed.

"Come on, Nathan," he said that first night. "You can
help fix up the bathroom for today's showerathon."

So, while Simon sat in his wheelchair in the middle of
the bathroom, and gave orders like Antilla the Hun, I took
his pajamas and dressing gown and put them on a chair
near the shower. Then I took another chair with very
short legs and put it in the shower, under the nozzle. Then
I got a towel and hung it on a hook at about knee height,
just outside the shower. Then I turned on the water,
while Simon kept putting his hand under it till it was just
right.

And then Simon pulled and pushed himself out of his
wheelchair till he was lying on the bathroom floor beside it.
"Help! Accident victim!" he moaned, and waved his arms
about. I wasn't too sure what to do. He really did look like
someone from a car smash, lying there with his legs all
floppy.

Simon grinned up at me. "Push off then," he said. "Can't
a man have any privacy in his own bathroom?"

I went out into the hallway and closed the bathroom door.
Mrs. Shaw was in Simon's room, turning down the covers

on his bed. His bed's got a rail all along one side so he can haul himself in and out of it.

"Listen to him," she said. "Can you tell what he's doing?"

There were flapping and thudding noises from the bathroom. "Simon taking off his clothes," said Mrs. Shaw. "It's easiest for him to lie on the floor and get undressed. He gets dressed the same way. Very unusual."

Next there were slithering noises. "Simon pulling himself into the shower and onto the chair. He has his shower sitting down. Very comfortable."

A sloshing noise. "Simon soaping and washing himself. Very messy."

A sudden moaning, howling, shrieking noise that made me jump. "Simon singing in the shower," said Mrs. Shaw. "Sorry, Nathan, I should have warned you. Very alarming."

More sloshing, then more slithering and a muffled rubbing noise. "Simon getting out of the shower and drying himself. Very complicated."

A second lot of flapping, thudding noises, with a muttering noise as well. "Simon putting his pajamas and dressing gown on. And getting the cord of his dressing gown in a tangle. Very predictable."

Then there was a shout. "Hey! Am I going to have to lie around here all night till someone comes?"

"Simon having finished his shower, asking to be helped back into his chair," said Mrs. Shaw. "Very polite."

I didn't stay the night at Simon's this Saturday. I had to come home to look after Fiona the Moaner and the brontosaurus while Mum went out to a concert with a teacher from her school. He's called Mr. O'Rourke—I reckon he's got his eye on Mum.

When we were packing up our role-playing stuff this afternoon, Haare asked, "Has that fifth-form girl said anything to you guys about role-playing games being evil?"

Jason, Todd, and I looked blank, but Simon piped up. "That very religious one? Yeah, she was trying to warn me off playing them a while back."

"What did she say?" Todd wanted to know.

"Oh, it was all a bit gross, man," Haare told him. "She was saying that playing games with demons and monsters in them is like dabbling in black magic. And the Bible warns us against such things."

"That right?" asked Jason. Jason's a good guy, but I wish he wouldn't let his mouth hang open when he says *that right?* "That right? So what did you say?"

"I told her the games we played weren't like that," Haare said. "We made up Orcs and Werekings and things out of the books, but we didn't pretend we were them. She said fair enough, so we kissed and made up, ho, ho."

"What did you tell her, Simon?" I asked him.

"I said to her, 'Look, there's this character in one game we're playing—he's got this fatal disease, and his legs are all withered, and his body's shrinking up, and he has to get around in this weird-looking wheelchair. You don't really believe I'm gonna become like that character, do you?' "

Jason, Todd, Haare, and I went home soon after that, but I couldn't help thinking about what Simon had said while I cleared the table after dinner. Fiona the Moaner was walking the dog. I'd told her that if she wanted to watch her cartoon program on TV, she had to walk the dog *and* dry the dishes. She moaned.

Some people make the mistake of treating Simon as if they know what's best for him. He looks so frail in his wheelchair that they feel sorry for him. They want to make all the decisions for him. But if Simon realizes people like that fifth-form girl, or anyone else, are trying to run his life for him, then man—it's them you're soon feeling sorry for.

CHAPTER
Five

Hey, Simon—," I began, when we met at the dairy on the way to school this morning.

"What?"

"What did one biscuit say when an elephant sat on the other biscuit?"

"I don't know."

"Crumbs!"

"What?"

"Crumbs. The other biscuit said *crumbs!*"

"Is that the whole joke?"

"Yeah. Well, it's Nelita's whole joke, actually."

"Tell her to go back to sleep, then."

Simon was in a foul mood for most of this morning. He reckons he hasn't had a decent night's sleep for a week. His arms and shoulders have been starting to feel strange. If he lies on one side in bed too long, that side goes dead and he loses feeling in it. And since his legs and hips are just about helpless, he can't turn over in bed properly. So his mum and dad, and even Kirsti, have been taking turns helping him roll over onto his other side four or five times a night.

"They wake me up doing it," he was complaining. "And I've hardly gotten back to sleep before they're turning me over again."

I almost said I wouldn't mind having Kirsti wake me up at any time, but I thought I'd better keep quiet.

Simon has to be turned over in bed every two hours or so because if he lies on the same side all the time, he may get pressure sores.

He has to be careful not to sit in exactly the same position for too long in his wheelchair, as well. He's got a polystyrene cushion under him, and three more little cushions to put in the small of his back and beside his hips, so they don't rub against the chair. He's got hardly any feeling left in his hips and thighs, so he doesn't even know if they are being rubbed.

You get pressure sores when too much weight presses against one part of your body for too long. The blood supply can't reach that part and your skin starts to turn red. If the pressure keeps up for a long time—say several hours a day for a week—then the skin starts turning bluey black, and the flesh under it starts dying.

That's why Simon has to check himself for signs every day, in a mirror low down on the Shaws' bathroom wall.

And that's why it's important that he doesn't sleep on the same side all night. He knows this, of course, but it doesn't stop him from grumbling about it.

I tried cheering him up by telling him that I had had a bad night, too. Fiona the Moaner caught her finger in a cupboard door yesterday afternoon and pinched her nail. From the fuss she made, you'd think her whole arm had come off.

She had to have the poor ickle finger bathed in antiseptic and hot water, and a bandage put on it. I suggested putting a red-hot poker on the wound. That's what they did in the Middle Ages to stop germs from spreading. Mum said there was a nasty streak in me that reminded her of my father. True enough—Dad does have a good sense of humor some-times.

Then Fiona woke us all up about ninety-five times in the night, calling out for Mum because her sore finger hurt, and Mum had to go and give her half an aspirin or loosen the bandage or whatever.

Her precious finger was still throbbing this morning, and would you believe it—Mum actually made a sling for the brat to put her hand in! She reckoned if Fiona kept her finger up high, it would stop the throbbing.

"If she wants to keep her finger up high, she should put a bit of Superglue on the end of it and then stick it on top of her head," Simon said.

"Or stick it in her ear," I suggested.

"Or up her nose," Simon grinned. "Aren't we nasty?"

But he still must have been in a bad mood, because

when Alex Wilson and two of his orangutan mates came biking past, Simon yelled out to them, "Hey, Wilson! Why aren't you wearing your helmet? Got nothing worth protecting?"

The three of them jerked their heads around and I felt a bit nervous. Making an enemy of Alex Wilson is not a recommended way of increasing your life expectancy. But when Alex saw it was Simon, he just said, "Zip your lip, Shaw," and kept on riding. I let out the deep breath I found I'd been holding.

Simon was still looking bad-tempered. "Silly fools," he muttered, more to himself than to me. "One crash and they could end up in a wheelchair."

The last bit was meant for me to hear, but I didn't say anything. There are times with Simon when it's best to keep your mouth shut. Sometimes he doesn't want somebody to talk to, but to talk *at*.

Things didn't get any better when we got to school, because the brakes on his wheelchair were playing up.

Simon's got two control levers on his new, electric-powered chair. The one for his right hand works the throttle. The lever by his left hand works the brakes. Push it forward, the left wheel brakes and the chair turns left. Pull it back, right brake and right turn. Hold it down, and both brakes are on at once.

Today the right brake kept sticking when Simon used it. So when he tried to turn into Room 18 for the first lesson, which was science with Mr. Packman, first the brake wouldn't work and then it wouldn't stop working. Simon ended up jammed against the corridor wall.

Just then, Mr. Packman came along on his way to class. "That's an interesting technique, Simon," he said. "Going to make your own doorway into the classroom, are you?" Simon muttered something that Mr. Packman decided he didn't hear.

"Nathan can give you a hand, I'm sure," added Mr. Packman as he walked into the classroom. "He's not just a pretty face."

So I pulled Simon's chair away from the wall and wrestled it around till it was pointing toward the doorway. Like I said before, his new wheelchair is *heavy!*

"That's enough! That's enough!" snapped Simon as soon as he was facing in the right direction. "I can manage!" He pulled the throttle lever and whirred into the classroom.

I followed behind him, feeling pretty annoyed myself. It wasn't my fault he'd gotten jammed against the wall. "Pardon me for living!" I grumbled.

Anyway, Simon should have been more careful. As soon as he was inside the classroom, his right brake jammed again. His chair turned and clipped the edge of Brady West's desk, jolting her elbow and making her smear green ink over a heading she'd been finishing.

"You stupid nerd!" exclaimed Brady. "Can't you watch where you're—" Then she saw it was Simon and shut up suddenly. Her neck started turning red.

Mr. Packman did the sensible thing. He told Simon off without making a big thing of it.

"Simon Aloysius Cholmondley Featherstonehaugh Shaw!"—no, those aren't Simon's real middle names—said Mr. Packman like a judge in a courtroom. "You are charged with driving a motorized vehicle, to wit, one wheelchair, without due care and attention. How do you plead—guilty or not innocent?"

Simon did the right thing, too. He answered, "Guilty, Your Honor. Guilty." Then he said to Brady, "Sorry, Brady. My fault."

Brady said, "That's all right, Simon. No worries." And hell, she gave him a special smile. That guy is such a smooth operator!

Simon cheered up a good deal after that. Who wouldn't! He seemed to have gotten something out of his system. And he cheered up even more after lunch when Haare and Jason showed him what they'd been making in metalwork.

Simon's already got a whole lot of gadgets and stickers on his wheelchair. Mr. Shaw's fitted an electric horn on it. The horn plays a tune, like the ones on those cars that go belting round the streets on Saturday nights.

The tune is the first part of "Dixie"—"Oh, I wish I was in the land of cotton—parp-a-parp parp-parp parp-a-parp parp *paarp-paarp!*" You can hear Simon using it when we're watching our school team play soccer, or when we're supporting our class relay team on Sports Day.

Once he started it going in assembly when Mr. Antill was yelling at everybody. "I *warn* you that I will *not* tolerate any more"—*parp-a-parp parp-parp!* Simon made out he'd touched the horn button accidentally, while Antilla the Hun gave him a look that would have melted steel.

He's also got stickers on the back of his chair that read KEEP CLEAR OF PROPELLERS and WARNING: VERTICAL TAKEOFF and I ♥ MY ROLLS-ROYCE.

This afternoon Haare and Jason came up carrying a couple of levers that they'd been making in metalwork without telling Simon. Haare was carrying them, actually. Jason had belted his fingers with the hammer while they were shaping them, and he was still nursing one hand.

They weren't real levers, just mock-up aluminum jobs to clip onto the side of Simon's wheelchair. They looked cool, though. Haare and Jason had cut them, painted them, and fitted plastic knobs to the ends. And they'd made metal signs to go with the levers. One read EMERGENCY EJECTOR SEAT and the other read TURBO ROCKET. They'd even spelled *emergency* and *ejector* right, which is pretty good for your average fourteen-year-old.

Simon was really pleased. He sat in the chair giving orders on exactly where he wanted the levers and the signs put, while Haare and Mr. Wood, the metalwork teacher—would you believe that name!—did the drilling and bolting, and Jason got the fingers of his other hand jammed in the spokes.

Everyone else was watching and cracking pathetic jokes about which lane Simon would be using on the motorway, and so on. It was a good feeling—the whole class came together.

Simon was in a rush to get home after school. Partly

because he wanted to show off his new levers and signs, and partly . . . well, partly because he was in a hurry to get to the toilet.

Usually he goes to the toilet just before he leaves for school. He needs his dad or mum to help lift him onto the seat now, and to wipe him afterward—he can't reach his hand right back behind himself any longer. Then he hangs on at school during the day. Sometimes he just hangs on and no more. "I could do with a *real* turbo rocket this afternoon," he said as we hurried off.

I was a bit disappointed. I didn't say anything to Simon, but I thought that if we hung around for a while, we might end up going home at the same time as Brady West. She lives just up the road from me. No such luck today.

But on the way home, we saw a fresh *Northern Spews* poster up outside the dairy: CHILD VICTIMS LIVE IN BRUTALIZED TERROR.

"Neat one!" said Simon. "Just like Antilla the Hun's math class."

He whirred off across the pedestrian crossing, and I wandered off up the sidewalk. Simon has good days and he has bad days. This one started off bad and ended up good.

CHAPTER
Six

This day didn't start off to be a very good one for me.

Fiona the Moaner and Mum were having an argument before school. Fiona didn't have a shower last night, and she didn't want to have one this morning or she'd be late meeting her repulsive little mates before school.

So she was whining and moaning, and Mum was laying down the law, saying, "A growing child should have a shower every day. It's simple hygiene."

Then I said I reckoned a bath would be better for Fiona, and I'd run her one, provided she promised to hold her breath under the water for twenty minutes. Mum didn't think this was very funny, for some reason.

Next, Fiona tried to get Mum's mind off the shower by

moaning that they were supposed to be having basketball trials at school that day, and her sneakers were falling to bits, and Mum had promised she was going to get her some new ones, and Mum hadn't, and now all the other kids were going to laugh at her—pause here to take deep breath before going into next moan.

I'll admit that Fiona's got a point about her sneakers. They'd split open at the toes near the end of last season, and I'd mended them for her with insulating tape. Trouble was, we didn't have much insulating tape left, so one shoe is held together with black and yellow strips while the other's got red and green on it. I keep telling her that at least she won't have any trouble remembering which shoe goes on which foot.

Anyway, she didn't have to start whining to Mum right then and there. Mornings are always a rush in our place, with Mum getting off to her school where she's a teacher's aide, and Fiona and me trying not to be late for ours. But, no, this morning is the time my little sister chooses, just when she should be taking the dog for his walk.

Mum got the strained look on her face that she gets when she's upset about something. "Sorry, honey," she said. "I just don't have the money this week."

"But I need them!" Fiona was moaning. No—she didn't say need, she said *neeeeeeed.*

"Look!" sighed Mum. "I've got to pay the power bill and the car insurance this week. You don't want to eat raw sausages and then have to walk to dancing lessons, do you?"

44

"Why don't you ask Dad to send you some money?" Fiona said. Oh dear. I got ready to hide under the table.

But Mum just looked sad and tired. "Your Dad's got his own life to build up again, love," she said. "He's going without things he's entitled to—even if he has complained about it, sometimes. We'll go and look for some sneakers next payday, I promise. Okay?"

Fiona put her arms around Mum's neck and gave her a slobbery kiss. I felt my stomach heave. "Thanks, Mummy," she cooed.

"Hey!" I said to her. "If you go and have a shower now, I'll walk the dog for you. Deal?"

Mum sent me a pleased look. Fiona seemed to be thinking about giving me a thank-you kiss, as well. Over my dead body! So I pointed my breakfast-toast-and-peanut-butter-and-honey-smeared knife at her till she went away.

"Thanks so much, Nathan," Mum said.

"No worries, Mum," I told her. I picked up the dog's leash and then side-stepped to avoid being knocked over by a barking brontosaurus that thundered past me. Mum and her bag hurried off to the corner where Mr. O'Rourke was waiting to give her a lift.

I didn't bother telling Mum that the route the dog drags me on in the mornings goes past Brady West's place, and there's always the chance she might be coming out on her way to school. There wasn't any sign of her today, though. Just as well, probably, when I noticed what the dog was doing to the flowering cherry tree by her neighbor's letter box.

45

Then, would you believe it, as I was coming out of our front gate after returning the dog to his cell, I bumped into Brady after all. Well, I didn't actually bump, because I stopped at the last moment, unfortunately. But it qualified as a near miss.

"Hi, Nathan," she said.

"Grnggrrga," I said.

"Saw you walking your dog before," she said.

"Fnnffwlkuh," I said.

"He's cute, isn't he?" she said.

Cute is not an adjective that I personally would use to describe our dog. I prefer *deformed* or *squalid* or *loathsome throwback*. But if Brady thought he was cute, then cute he was. I gave her a slow smile and a sophisticated, man-of-the-world reply. "Aw yeah," I said.

Brady has blue eyes with a tiny golden fleck in the right one. Not that I've been staring, mind you. She's got long, light-colored hair that she wears pinned up behind, and her neck looks all soft and smooth. Jason's bottom jaw hangs open even lower than usual when he looks at her.

By the time we got down the road a bit further, I was making quite smooth conversation. At any rate, I'd got past *grnggrrga* and *oh yeah*.

Simon was waiting at the dairy. I could hear him telling some primary-school kids that yeah, those were real turbo rockets on his wheelchair, and yeah, that was a real emergency ejector seat, in case his chair got stuck in a piranha-infested swamp or something.

He gave me his know-it-all grin as Brady and I approached. "Wondered what had kept you," he said.

Then my so-called friend proceeded to hog the conversation with Brady all the rest of the way to school. He talked, and she laughed at his jokes, and I walked along beside them, getting more and more hacked off.

To make things worse, Nelita Travers caught up with us and insisted on talking to me, saying she wished she was as good at science as I was, and telling me more gross jokes like, "Why didn't the butterfly go to the ball? Because it was a mothball." Nelita's little and dark, and okay, she's nice-looking. But not as nice-looking as Brady.

By the time we got to school, it was my turn to be in a foul mood. We had English first lesson, and I hardly spoke to Simon as we went in. He's always in the limelight—people are always paying attention to him. Let him see what it's like to be ignored for a bit.

Simon doesn't sit at a desk in class. The wheels on his wheelchair won't fit under the desk properly, and now that he's having trouble with his arms and shoulders, it's difficult for him to lean forward and do his work on a desktop.

At home for meals, he takes off his wheelchair arms—they just lift out on rods—and he drives himself in so his legs are right under the table. At school, he uses a special desk that the hospital made for him. It's a hinged board like a small tray that folds down against the side of the chair when he's not using it. There's a rim around the sides of it to stop ballpoints and things from rolling over the edge.

At the end of the tray nearest to Simon's body, there's even a small hollow where he can rest his elbow to keep it steady while he writes. His arm gets tired quickly, and it sometimes starts giving sudden jerks and quivers. "Hello, my arm's ringing me up," he says.

"Okay, you lot," said Ms. Kidman when we were all sitting down, and Jason had finished rubbing the shin that he'd banged against the desk leg, and Alex Wilson had finished thumping the guys on either side of him. "Pay attention. Anyone found talking will be shot and then given detention."

Ms. Kidman is a choice teacher. She makes you work, but she makes English enjoyable. Partly it's the interesting things she gets us to do, like writing your own words for songs, or the class video we're going to start making soon. And partly it's because in her class you feel that what you write and what you say gets treated with respect. It makes you feel like you're worth listening to.

The only time I've ever seen Ms. Kidman get angry was when Jason gave a wrong answer, a *very* wrong answer, and Brady—yeah, Brady—whispered "Geek!" to him.

"The only geek in this class is a person who sneers at those who try, and who hasn't got the guts to try herself, Brady West!" Ms. Kidman said. She didn't raise her voice, but you felt as if someone had opened the door of a deep freeze and icy air was blowing past you. Brady's cheeks turned an interesting ripe tomato color.

"Right, will you turn to the Personal Writing part of your

folders, please," Ms. Kidman asked this morning. Groans from the class.

"No suicide attempts, please," grinned Ms. Kidman. "I don't want any nasty stains on my floor. Anyway, you're not going to write an essay." Sighs of relief from the class.

"Some of you apparently heard a rumor that you were going to write a story about being yourself. Well, you're not." Murmurs of pleasure from the class.

"You're going to write a *poem* about being yourself instead." Groans and whimpering noises from the class. I looked around to see if Fiona the Moaner had somehow come to the wrong school.

But as usual with Ms. Kidman, it got interesting. She drew a series of circles on the board, one inside the other. "Eccentric circles," she announced.

"*Con*centric circles, Ms. Kidman," Simon corrected her. Ms. Kidman blew him a kiss and got Nelita to take him a jelly bean from the jar on her desk. You'd think that sort of thing would be childish and stupid at high school, but Ms. Kidman knows exactly how to do it.

"These circles are the layers of yourself," she said. "The skins you cover yourself with, to protect you from the world." A classful of onions, I thought.

"Inside those skins, those circles, is the real you," Ms. Kidman went on. "It's a you that you're very nervous about letting people see, because you all feel that there are things about you, fears and problems and embarrassments, that other people will laugh at. Right?"

There were nods from the class. Even Alex Wilson

nodded—or maybe his brain rolled from the back of his skull to the front.

"And the funny thing is, if you ever do tell someone about the fears at the center of your circles, they often turn out to have the same sorts of fears and worries too, and you feel better for having told them. Right?"

More nods. The Wilson brain rolled backward and forward again.

"Okay, and that's one of the things poetry can do," Ms. Kidman continued. "Poetry can let you get your fears out into the open, so you can share them with yourself and feel better. And maybe share them with others—but only if you want to. Poetry written in this class is allowed to stay private."

Then Ms. Kidman got us to scribble down on rough paper the sorts of places that make us feel lonely or depressed. She asked us about times when we've felt bad. Was it during winter weather? Or blue summer weather? Or when we've had to go home to an unhappy house? Or when we've had to come to English? No one laughed—we were all getting too wrapped up in the possibilities. There were more questions: Was it worse having other people around when you felt miserable? What colors do you associate with feeling depressed and sad? What movements—are you sitting still or wandering around?

"Here's a possible beginning," said Ms. Kidman. On the board, she wrote two words: *I am* . . .

"Now just spend the next five minutes seeing if any of the things you've scribbled down can build into sentences or lines," said Ms. Kidman as she put down her chalk. "Don't worry if the lines don't fit together. Don't worry about whether it makes sense. Don't worry about rhyme. Just go for the middle of those circles."

The classroom was silent except for ballpoints scribbling and scratching out. Even Alex Wilson was writing. Mind you, he's probably written quite a lot of poetry already, on bathroom walls.

I was pleased to hear the *don't worry about rhyme* bit, because the only words I could think of to rhyme with Brady West were *lady's vest*, and that didn't seem likely to win a Nobel prize. I looked across to wink at Simon the way we often do in class, but he was busy writing. Then I remembered I was in a bad mood with him anyway.

When the five minutes were up, Ms. Kidman read us some lines she'd been scribbling too. They were about how scared she got when she faced a class for the first time. I'd never thought of teachers getting scared.

"Okay, now remember that poetry is allowed to stay private," Ms. Kidman said. "But is there anyone who'll read what they've written down? Your fears can't be any sillier than mine."

Nobody wanted to go first, of course, but after a couple of seconds hands started going up. That shows how people feel sort of worthwhile in Ms. Kidman's class.

Lana Patu had a good one about her nana dying and the shock of seeing her father cry. Nelita had a surprisingly sensible one about being afraid of nuclear war. Haare had a really hilarious one on being scared he was going to fart in assembly. "Great! Great!" said Ms. Kidman. "The little funny fears can be as bad as the big ones."

Then she looked over toward our side of the room, and I saw that Simon's hand was up. "Yes, Simon? You've got one?"

Simon took up the sheet of paper from the desk-tray on his wheelchair. He held it for a second, then he read.

I am here in the bright summer days.
Outside, the world gleams and glitters;
Inside, my chair and I watch leaves in the sun,
Or listen to distant laughing voices.
There, boys swim, surf, smile at girls;
Here, I sit in my chair and read,
Or watch old midday movies,
Or push myself from room to room.
When my friends break in from their shining worlds,
Part of me breaks, too.

When he'd finished the last line, Simon put the paper back down on the tray and looked straight ahead.

The guys in the class were all staring at their desks or at their feet. The girls were doing much the same. Nelita and Lana, I think it was, made little swallowing noises. Every bit of bad temper and jealousy I'd ever felt about Simon vanished down the cracks in the floorboards.

Ms. Kidman was great. She was as silent as the rest of us for a few seconds. Then she spoke very quietly.

"Every so often, a poem will say something that you know straight away you'll never forget, no matter how long you live. I think we've heard one of those this morning. Thank you from all of us, Simon."

And the bell rang for the end of the lesson.

CHAPTER
Seven

I rang Simon up that night because I thought he should have the bad news broken to him gently. "Fiona's done another drawing for me to give you," I told him.

"Oh hell," groaned the voice on the other end of the line. "What's it show this time?"

"It looks to me like a mad strangler creeping up behind his victim," I said. "But she reckons it's me pushing you in your chair."

"Someday, Nathan, that sister of yours is going to produce great works of art."

"Maybe, but this isn't the day."

"Fair enough," agreed Simon. Then he said, "You were doing all right with Nelita on the way to school this morning. I couldn't get a word in."

"*I* couldn't get a word in, either!" I told him. "Not to Nelita or to you and Brady. *She* was the one I wanted to talk to."

Simon chuckled. "You haven't got a chance, boy. Any girl with taste is going to prefer me. I've got good looks, intelligence, sparkling conversation, a great personality—"

"Modesty?" I suggested.

"That, too," he agreed. "And anyway, a girl is naturally going to be impressed by a guy who's got his own set of wheels."

I laughed. "Wait till your battery runs down again and she has to push you."

"Anyway," Simon went on, "starting next week, you won't have any competition for a while."

An uneasy feeling crawled down the middle of my back. He was making out that he was joking, but his voice sounded flat.

"What's the story?" I asked.

"I'm going back into hospital for a while," Simon said. "Dr. Mehta wants to do some more tests on me. I reckon I've had more tests at hospital than in Antilla the Hun's math class."

I wasn't sure what to say. If you tell Simon you're sorry, he bites your head off. If you try telling him everything'll be all right, he accuses you of talking crap, which is true. So I just asked him about it.

"Did Dr. Mehta say how long you'll be there?"

"About four days, she thinks. Maybe a bit longer. She said they've got a new drug that helps circulation, and they're thinking of working out a dosage for me. Sounds like a *Northern Spews* headline, doesn't it? Teenager on Drug Trip While Doctor Watches."

Because Simon's muscles are gradually wasting away from the muscular dystrophy, and because he can't do much exercise—except for his physical therapy, which he bunks if he's feeling lazy—he's always got a problem with not getting enough blood round his body. He takes tablets that are meant to make his arteries and capillaries expand so the blood can get around more easily. "If you ever get blocked drains, just chuck one of my tablets down them," he says. "That'll clear things, no problem."

"You haven't had to go into hospital for a long time," I said over the phone.

"I was in this time last year, remember? That was for another drug. I've had the drugs, now all I need is the sex and the rock 'n' roll. You know, like in the song, "Sex, Drugs, and Rock 'n' Roll"?

"Yeah, I know. Sounds better when other people sing it, though."

"Watch it, boy. I'll tell Fiona to do some drawings for *you*."

"When did you say you were going in?"

"Sunday afternoon. Should be out about Thursday. Just think—I'll miss three periods of math. Oh dear, how sad, never mind. Anyway, I'll be at school the rest of this week. I'll give you another lesson on how to chat up Brady to-morrow morning, if you like."

"Ha very ha. See ya, Simon."

"See ya, Nathan."

We hung up. I'd made a secret promise to myself after the English lesson that morning that I was going to be kind to everyone, including dumb animals. So I went off to help Fiona the Moaner with her science project. She's doing *Trees*. Since she's such a little sap, and since I'm trying to turn over a new leaf with her, it seems appropriate.

Once when we were in the third form, we had a discussion in social studies about hospitals—whether they did much good or whether it was better to be treated at home if you could.

Some of the girls said they were going to have their babies at home. Alex Wilson asked, "In the kitchen or the dining room?" and was given an essay to write by Mr. Rata. I thought it was quite clever, actually. Probably the wittiest thing Alex has said in his life.

Then someone asked Simon what he thought of hospitals. Since he'd spent a lot of time there, I suppose it was a reasonable question, though you might as well ask Jason what he thinks of the school's sick bay—he's in there at least once a week.

Simon looked blank for a moment. While he looked blank, Mr. Rata looked nervous. Some teachers feel that way with Simon. He can come out with some fairly disturbing things. He's probably too truthful for his own good.

Then he said, "I don't *like* being there. But they found out what was wrong with me, and that was a relief, in a way. And they made me realize I was pretty lucky, really."

I know I wasn't the only one thinking *lucky?* Nelita did us all a favor and asked Simon what he meant.

"Oh, we had kids in the children's ward who had a much worse time than me. There were two of them with bad cerebral palsy—that's where the part of your brain that controls your movements is damaged, and you can't stop your head or your body from twitching and jerking."

"Is that like being spastic?" someone else asked. Alex Wilson started to go, "Duh! Spas—" then shut up when he saw that Mr. Rata was watching him.

"Yeah, that's right," said Simon, who was enjoying taking over the lesson. "Spastics have a sort of cerebral palsy. They are not mentally retarded or anything. Some of the kids in our ward were really clever, even though you couldn't understand what they were saying till you got used to them. But they couldn't control their body movements. One cerebral palsy kid I knew had to wear a crash helmet all the time because his head kept banging and jerking against things. And then there were the spina bifida kids."

"My cousin's got that," Becky Klenner said. "She has to lie on her front all the time. She's got this really weird wheelchair. It's not like yours, Simon. It's like a bed with a motor and wheels."

"Who knows what spina bifida is?" Mr. Rata interrupted. Nobody did, except for Simon and Becky.

"It means you're born with some of your backbone missing," Becky said. "Your spinal cord and the nerves and things hang right out of your back."

"It's not always as bad as that," Simon corrected her.

Mr. Rata seemed to decide the discussion was going fine without him. He found a spare chair and made himself comfortable.

"We had one spina bifida kid in our ward who was like that," Simon went on. "But there were other ones who looked quite ordinary, except they couldn't walk or sit up. Some of them were waiting for an operation where the doctors slice a sort of canal in your back for the spinal cord to go in." A few kids in the class turned white or green at this stage. "Then they build an artificial backbone round it. If the operation's okay, some spina bifida kids can walk —after a fashion."

"How long were you in hospital for, Simon?" Nelita likes asking questions almost as much as she likes cracking gross jokes. Brady and a few other kids rolled their eyes, but Simon didn't seem to mind.

"I was in for eighteen months, on and off, till they'd made sure I had muscular dystrophy, and they could work out my physical therapy and drugs. They soon found out I wasn't any good on crutches."

"Why?" Todd Martin asked.

"Because I didn't have enough strength in my legs," said Simon. He stopped and looked pleased with himself for taking over the class. "If you swing along on crutches, your legs have to be strong enough to land on. Mine weren't. Instead of going heave-thump, I kept going heave-crash. Anyway, crutches are useless in the wet—they slip on wet floors and sidewalks. I was always skidding all over."

"Simon—?" began Lana Patu.

59

"Yes, Lana?" said Simon, exactly like a teacher. Everyone laughed, including Mr. Rata, who folded his arms and settled deeper in his chair.

"Do you still see any of the kids from the hospital? Are any of them still there?"

"Oh yeah," Simon told her. "Some of them won't ever leave. They need hospital equipment and doctors all the time. I see them whenever I go back, and we phone one another up and send Christmas cards and stuff. There was another guy there at the same time as me—he had muscular dystrophy too, worse than me, and we had the beds next to each other for nearly a year. I used to go and see him a lot after I first got out."

"Is he still in hospital?" asked Lana. I thought for a moment she was going to say "Please, sir" first, Simon was so much in charge of the discussion. "Or is he back home like you?"

Simon looked blank again for a second. "Neither," he said. "He's dead."

There was a sudden scraping of a chair over on one side of the room. Mr. Rata had unfolded his arms and was standing up again.

CHAPTER
Eight

I hate dogs," Fiona the Moaner started saying at lunchtime today.

"You hate dogs?" replied Mum. "Oh well, I suppose every girl should have a hobby."

"Well, I hate our dog," Fiona moaned on. "When I take him for walks he always pulls too hard on the leash and does wees on trees." The girl may make a poet yet.

"There's no need to be catty about our dog," I said.

"Perhaps he's hounding Fiona to despair?" Mum suggested.

"I think she's just barking up the wrong tree," I added.

Fiona stamped off to her room and slammed the door. The dog, who always follows her round the house—I think they both have the same IQ—went and lay down in the hallway outside.

Fiona's been in a foul mood for the last few days, ever since a letter arrived from Dad, asking if I'd like to stay with him in the holidays. She went during the last holidays, so she knows it's my turn. But that doesn't stop her from whining.

Funny thing is, I'm not all that sure I want to go and stay with Dad. Oh, I'm fond of him and all. I was more upset than Fiona when he and Mum split up—she was too little to understand much, then. But it's sort of embarrassing, seeing him for just a few days at a time. Things are always awkward at first. He's so polite, and lets me do anything I want. It's better later on, when he starts telling me off the way a normal parent does. And he's always asking all these questions about Mum. Hell, how do I know whether she's feeling all right about herself? I have enough trouble trying to work out how *I* feel about myself.

Since it was Sunday, I went round to Simon's after lunch. This is the afternoon he's going into hospital, and I wanted to give him some advice on checking out the nurses. We didn't have role-playing at his place yesterday. Jason walked into a tree branch while he was mowing his lawn and had to spend the afternoon lying down with a bleeding nose.

Kirsti opened the door and gave me a big smile. "Hi, Nathan. How are you?"

"Mffnwhrr," I said. There's something about Kirsti and Brady West that drags all my vocabulary down to the same level.

"I've just washed my hair," she said. "That's why it's looking all rat-tails and horrible like this."

Now it so happens that she said exactly the same thing to me one Sunday afternoon when I'd been round at the Shaws', and I had decided that if she ever said anything like that again, I'd have a really suave reply ready. I'd tell her that she reminded me of a girl who'd just stepped from a mountain pool on some tropical island. Here was my chance.

"Aw no," I said. "Doesn't look too bad."

Kirsti laughed. "Thanks, Nathan," she said. "Simon's in his room."

I kicked myself down the hall to Simon's bedroom. He was tidying up his floor. "Mum and Dad said I wasn't going off to hospital and leaving this place looking like a pigsty," he grumbled. "I said they could turn a couple of pigs loose in it while I was gone and charge them rent. But parents never listen."

Since Simon can't bend down in his chair to pick things up, he tidies his floor with a long pair of tongs that Mr. Shaw made for him. The hospital gave him a little fishing net on a pole to use, but after Mrs. Shaw caught her foot in it twice when Simon left it lying on the floor, she said he had to get rid of that something-or-other net, or else she'd serve *him* up in batter for dinner.

So now Simon uses the tongs instead. He moves things with them like I move things when I'm tidying my room. He picks them up, looks at them vaguely for a while, then puts them down again somewhere else.

He has to vacuum his room, too. Since the switch is too far down on the wall for Simon to reach, his parents or Kirsti plug the cleaner in for him and turn it on. Then he whirrs around in his chair, dragging the cleaner after him.

The Shaws have done a lot of things to make it easier for Simon to get around inside and outside the house. They've put in concrete ramps up to the back door and the front door. They used to have one at the back door only, but then they thought, what if there's a fire or earthquake or something, and Simon has to try and get out the front door? He won't be able to get down the steps. So they had a second ramp built.

At the bottom of the back-door ramp, there's a wooden post with a stiff-bristle brush hanging from it. It's for Simon to brush off any dirt or leaves or traces of our dog that he might have gotten on his wheels before he goes inside. Simon says they should put a notice on the post. Other houses sometimes have a sign saying Please Wipe Your Feet. He wants one that says Please Wipe Your Wheels.

Looking after Simon has cost Mr. and Mrs. Shaw a lot of money. Simon says they never talk about it, but he knows. "I'm a dear little boy in more ways than one," he says.

The hospital pays for the wheelchair and crutches and the doctor and his physical therapy, and it paid to have the electric hoist put in the Shaws' van that lifts Simon in and out.

Before the hoist, they had a long aluminum ramp that they stored inside the van. Trouble was, once they had the ramp in position, Simon didn't always wait for someone to get up into the van and help him down. He'd just roll over to the edge and tear down the ramp, yelling "*Banzai! Banzai!*"

After a couple of near misses with pedestrians in the shopping center, and after Mr. Shaw decided he was going to end up bent over like a staple from pushing Simon back up the ramp, they got the hoist instead.

But the Shaws had to pay the extra cost when they sold their car and bought the big van to carry Simon's wheelchair. And they've paid for the ramps and other things they've done around the house.

One time Mr. Shaw had the chance of being promoted to another branch of his stock brokerage firm in a different town, but he said no. The house they were in was the right place for them and Simon. So he gave up the extra money he would have gotten from being promoted. I bet Dad would have done the same if it had been me or Fiona.

Remember Mrs. Mason—the Shaws' baby-sitter–neighbor, and the second link in the information chain?

Once Mrs. Mason asked Mrs. Shaw if she didn't miss being able to travel and go overseas, and to do the sorts of things that people sometimes can when their kids have grown up a bit, and when they're in a good job like Mr. Shaw is.

Mrs. Shaw said no. She felt that living with Simon had taught her to appreciate how special ordinary things were. She'd learned to look at the leaves on trees and the shapes flames make in the fire. Being with Simon had even taught her to enjoy watching the grass grow.

Just as well she doesn't live up our street. Our dog's

killed most of the grass there, and now he's working on the trees. And if there was a fire burning when he was passing by . . .

When Simon had finished moving all the stuff on his floor from the left side of the room to the right side, and then back to the left side again, it was time for the Shaws to take him to the hospital. He had a couple of bags already packed—a small one with pajamas and a dressing gown, and a big one with role-playing games.

"I'm going to work out some plays for Clash of the Battle-Apes that'll leave you guys for dead," he said.

I'm not a great fan of the Battle-Apes game, actually. Whenever we're playing it, I can't get this picture of Alex Wilson out of my mind.

The Shaws asked me if I'd like to ride along in the van while they took Simon to the hospital. Then they'd drop me off on their way home. "You and Kirsti can keep an eye on Simon in the back," said Mrs. Shaw. "Tie him down if you need to."

Oh well, I thought, if Kirsti's going to be coming along, she'll probably appreciate some witty conversation. "I'll just ring up Mum first," I said.

"Fine," said Mrs. Shaw. "You know where the phone is."

"Of course he does," Simon told her. "It's on the end of the cord."

Mum was perfectly happy for me to go. "Give Simon my love," she ordered. "And you'd better warn him to build his strength up—Fiona's doing another drawing for when we come to visit him." Then she paused for a moment and said, "You're a neat kid, Nathan," and hung up.

Of course I'm a neat kid! Could anyone doubt it for a microsecond? Maybe a few people should pass the news on to Brady West.

Simon steered his wheelchair onto the platform of the van hoist and announced, "We have ignition sequence." And as the hoist began rising up, he called, "We have a liftoff! We have a liftoff!"

I helped Kirsti climb into the back—wowee!—and we were away laughing.

On the way to the hospital, Simon talked about the other times he'd been there—especially the eighteen months when he was in primary school, and they were diagnosing and trying to control his MD. I think he was quite excited about going back to see some of the people he knew. I felt a bit jealous for a minute, till I remembered the resolution I'd made after that poetry business at school last week.

I think Kirsti must have been feeling a bit down about Simon having to go in again. She just sat and didn't say much.

"We used to have these wheelchair races," Simon was saying. "Especially this guy Kevin and me. I told you about him—he was the one who had cerebral palsy and had to wear a crash helmet all the time."

"Yeah, I remember," I said. "So he was a wheelchair racer in a crash helmet? He must have looked the real thing.

Did the winner spray a bottle of champagne over the crowd like they do on television?"

"I tried it with a can of Coke after I won one race," Simon said. "The nurses made me spend the afternoon wiping down the walls with a wet tea towel."

"Where did you race?" I asked him. "Up and down the wards? You'd have to be careful, surely? Someone could have an accident and end up in hospital."

"Get real!" Simon replied. "No, we used to go out in the car park. The other muscular dystrophy guy, Sione, was on crutches, and he'd stand up at one end and watch out for anything coming. I just had my old chair then, the one I had to push. So I used to be able to get in front for the first half, down to where Sione was standing. But then my arms would start getting tired on the way back. Kevin always passed me. He used to look hilarious—his head and arms twitching, and his chair whirring, and him laughing."

"So his motor beat your muscles," I said.

"Yeah, most of the time," said Simon. "But there was one time when his throttle jammed, eh? He couldn't slow down or turn or anything. He went straight past Sione and out the end of the car park, and headed for the main gates. Sione was yelling "Stop! Stop!" and hobbling along after him on his crutches. I came after Sione, pushing as hard as I could on my wheels, and yelling 'Stop! Stop!' too. Man, it must have looked weird!"

"What happened to the escaped chair?" I wanted to know.

"Oh, a couple of nurses coming on duty met Kevin as he

was starting to go through the gates and grabbed him. Just as well—he might've been halfway across the Sahara by now." Simon was silent for a bit, remembering. "Kevin was a neat guy. So was Sione, but he died when he was about twelve."

The van swung down the hospital drive and stopped at the main entrance. Mrs. Shaw opened the back doors. Kirsti didn't need me to give her a hand out—damn! Simon came down to earth on the hoist. He looked a bit nervous.

The hospital smelled like hospitals always do—like polish and some sort of antiseptic. It sounded the way hospitals always do, too—like shoes squeaking on linoleum and uniforms swishing.

Since they were expecting Simon, we went straight to his ground-floor ward. We must have looked like Mafia bodyguards as we all marched along behind him in his chair. A pretty Indian woman in a white coat came out of a door near the ward entrance. "Hi, Simon," she said.

"Hi, Dr. Mehta," said Simon. "What's for dinner?"

Dr. Mehta laughed. "I knew you'd be asking that, so I found out. Fish and chips, followed by fresh fruit salad."

"Choice!" exclaimed Simon. "Hey, I should come here more often."

Dr. Mehta laughed again. Then she and Mr. and Mrs. Shaw and Simon went off together to organize his bed and things. "I must talk to you about the Paritai Home for Disabled Children," she was saying to Simon's parents. "I think they might be able to offer Simon a place there for a week of the school holidays."

Kirsti and I sat in the ward waiting room. What did we do? We waited.

We talked, too. Kirsti's easy to talk to. She's a bit like Ms. Kidman. She makes you feel that the things you say are worth listening to. I told her about going to see Dad in the holidays, and the horrors of life with Fiona the Moaner, and what it was like down in the swamps of the fourth form. She talked about how different the teachers were when you were a seventh former, and how friendly everyone was to one another, because it's the last year of school. "There are a lot of nice kids in the seventh form this year, especially the girls," she said.

Then she grinned at me. "Mind you, there's some pretty nice girls in the fourth form, too, I believe. There's Lana Patu, and Nelita Travers, and someone called . . . Brady East, is that right?"

A polished, elegant, grown-up reply leaped to my lips. "Uurrnghh," I said.

Simon was in his chair beside his bed when Mr. Shaw finally fetched us along to see him. There were two beds in the room, but the other bed was empty. A nurse who didn't look any older than Kirsti was flipping through some of Simon's role-playing books with him. "Have a good four days in the maximum-security wing," he told me. "Think of me during math."

"I'll save all the assignments for you," I promised him. "See ya Friday. No, I'll come in on Tuesday. Mum and

Fiona want to come and visit you, too. And I almost forgot, Fiona's doing another drawing." A hunted sort of look crossed Simon's face.

I felt a bit envious of Simon on the way home in the van—pretty nurses, four days off school, everyone fussing over him. Then I noticed how quiet all the Shaws were.

CHAPTER
Nine

On Tuesday, Mum, Fiona, and I went to visit Simon in hospital. Jason was supposed to be coming with us, too, but there'd been this argument between his finger and a hot Bunsen burner in science.

Fiona took Simon a drawing that seemed to show a head growing out of a tray, but that Simon guessed with a bit of help was a portrait of him sitting up in his hospital bed. I took him the latest headline from the *Northern Spews*— More Like Gorilla Than Man, Victim Sobs.

"Alex Wilson's in the news a lot these days," Simon said.

Then on Thursday at school, Kirsti stopped me in the corridor while I was on my way to math. I never mind being stopped on my way to math, and I particularly never mind being stopped by Kirsti. For one thing, it does your reputation no end of good when people see you being chatted up by a seventh-form girl.

"Simon won't be coming home today," she said.

"Why not?" I'm quicker than a computer circuit with these probing questions.

"He hurt his shoulder during physical therapy. Stupid idiot—he's got this new exercise to help his arm muscles, and he did it harder than he was supposed to. He half dislocated his shoulder. They put it back, but he's got to stay in hospital for a few more days. He wants to know if you and the others would like to go over there for role-playing on Saturday afternoon."

"Uh-huh," I said. I'm quick with the replies, too.

Lana Patu, Nelita Travers, and Becky Klenner told us to give Simon their love, which was pretty nice of them. I hung around a bit to let Brady say the same, but she must have been feeling too shy. She's leaving for school at a different time these days. I haven't managed to intercept her for a while.

So on Saturday afternoon, Haare, Todd, and Jason came round to our place, where the dog slobbered over them, and we sorted out some role-playing stuff to take over to the hospital.

One of the many, many drawbacks of having a small sister is the things she comes up with when your friends are around. Sure enough, just as we were getting ready to head off for the hospital, Fiona the Moaner starts squeaking, "Don't forget your bicycle helmet, Nathan." Mum was there, or else I'd have replied with a few things that Fiona shouldn't forget—like the danger she's in when she tries ordering me about.

She's always been like that. When I was in primary school, I was heading out the gate with Haare one Sunday morning, and Fiona came rushing down the path after us, yelling, "Don't forget, Mummy says you have to wear an undershirt and be careful crossing the main road!" Haare fell all over the place laughing, of course, while I just about vanished in a plume of steam. It's even worse when she's reminding you of something you really have forgotten, like the bicycle helmet.

At the hospital, Haare, Todd, and I formed a protective cordon around Jason, so that he wouldn't bump into any sharp objects such as nurses. We marched him along the corridor to Simon's room. Simon was in his chair, with his right arm in a sling. I thought he looked a bit pale, but he perked up when we came in. "Meet the one-armed bandit," he said.

Simon's not the only guy getting medical treatment at the moment. Haare has to have an operation over the holidays to pull a wisdom tooth that's growing in crooked. Then he's going to get braces on his teeth.

So of course we all spent five minutes seeing who could make the worst jokes about how someone as thick as Haare could have any wisdom teeth. It filled in time while we were setting up the game, and it helped us get over the awkwardness you feel when you're making a polite visit to someone.

Simon told us all the hospital horror stories while we played Barbarians of the Black Star. We had to throw the dice for him because of the sling on his arm. Kirsti was right—he was a stupid idiot to do his exercises too hard. He knows his muscles are weak, and getting weaker, and that he could easily dislocate something.

"You have to be awake for breakfast at half past seven!" he said. "Even on Saturday! And you're not allowed to have the television on any later than ten o'clock at night in case it disturbs the other kids!"

"That right?" asked Jason, and hung his mouth open three notches.

I shook my head. "Ten o'clock! How gross, man!" I didn't let on that Mum won't let me watch television any later than that, either.

"Any decent-looking girls in the ward?" Haare and his big grin wanted to know.

Simon shook his head. "Nah," he replied. "I'm the oldest here this time. The rest are all little ankle biters. There's only a couple I remember from last year."

"Many visitors?" I asked. I was actually wondering if Brady might have been to see him.

But he thought I was talking about the other kids in the hospital. "Oh yeah," he said. "It's like Friday night downtown half the time. Some of them have mothers staying in here nearly all day. Fathers, too, now that there're more of them out of work. Hey, I reckon that's one really useful thing I do! Just think of all the doctors and nurses and therapists and wheelchair makers and drug manufacturers I make work for. I'm really helping to keep unemployment down."

"That right?" asked Jason, and he lowered his jaw to the fourth notch. The rest of us sighed.

"Don't let your mouth hang open, Jason," Todd warned him. "They might think you're waiting for an anesthetic."

"That ri—?" began Jason, then closed his mouth in a hurry.

"There's one little kid who's been here for months," Simon said. "She's got spina bifida. Her parents live miles away, and they only see her at the weekends. She's quite a reasonable little sprog—when you consider she's a female ankle biter. One of the nurses was telling me that this kid's got an uncle and aunt here in town, and a couple of cousins about her age. And this uncle! Oh, you wouldn't believe it, man!"

"Believe what?" asked Haare. We were all looking at Simon, and I realized suddenly how angry he was. The corners of his mouth were all white and squeezed-looking.

"This kid's uncle doesn't ever come to see her, and he won't let her aunt or her cousins come to see her, either. He reckons he's not taking any risks of them catching something. Catching spina bifida! Hell, how can anyone be so thick!"

"It's your turn," Todd said, passing the dice to Jason. I think he was feeling a bit embarrassed at the state Simon was getting in.

Jason was starting to shake the dice when Simon burst out again.

"I read once about a taxi driver who wouldn't take a woman with cerebral palsy where she wanted to go, because he didn't want any disease in his taxi. But this uncle . . . Shit!" Simon suddenly slammed the hand of his undislocated arm down hard on his wheelchair tray. "Geeks like that shouldn't be allowed to have kids of their own!"

I think we all jumped. I know Jason did. The dice he was shaking shot out of the hospital glass we were using and bounced onto the floor. Jason lurched after them and hit his forehead on the side of Simon's bed. He jerked upright again, saying something that Alex Wilson would have recognized, caught the glass with his elbow, and sent it ricocheting against the wall. As he made a grab for it, all the role-playing books cascaded onto the floor to join the dice.

It took Haare, Todd, and me a minute or so to pick up everything, including Jason. When we looked at Simon, he wasn't white in the face anymore. He was pink and shaking.

"Okay!" he said. "Okay! And I reckon there are some guys in this room who shouldn't ever be allowed to have kids, either. Not unless you want the human race to destroy itself!"

CHAPTER

Ten

We were making our video in English when Simon arrived back at school.

"I know it's the last week of term, but we can get a couple of scenes done," Ms. Kidman said. "Then you can spend the holidays deciding whether you deserve an Oscar."

"An Oscar?" asked Nelita. "You mean an Oscar like the Hollywood stars get?"

"No," said Ms. Kidman. "I mean Oscar as in overacted, sloppy, careless, and ridiculous. Now for goodness' sake, let's get organized!"

You can't really blame Ms. Kidman for getting her liver in a quiver. Making videos is a tricky business where our school is concerned.

Just last year, the sixth form—Kirsti was in it, that's how

I know—decided they were going to make a video of the Shakespeare play they were studying. It's called *Hamlet*, and there's one scene in it where the chief dude is watching a couple of grave diggers working in a new grave. The play is set way back in the days before color television, so I suppose people had to find different ways of having fun then.

The easiest place to dig a grave on our school grounds is the long-jump pit. The sixth form got a bit carried away and dug out the whole pit. Then it rained, and next thing you know, there's a new, oblong freshwater lake on the grounds. Mr. Johnston lined the sixth form up in front of the pit and said they could either put the dirt back in it, or put themselves in it.

Then it turned out this *Hamlet* play needed some human bones and skulls. These aren't exactly easy to get hold of. Luckily, one of the sixth-form girls lived on a farm, and she said she'd see what she could manage. When the video was finished, everybody could see what she'd managed. The video should have been called *Piglet*, not *Hamlet*.

So Ms. Kidman insisted that our video was going to be properly organized before we started. We'd decided on the story. Or rather, Ms. Kidman and all the girls in the class had decided on the story. It was going to be about the women's suffragette movement.

The suffragettes weren't women who made men suffer, as Haare pretended to believe. They were the women who first demanded the right to vote, and they had all these pretty impressive demonstrations and marches to make their opinions public. Good on them, I reckon.

"Fair enough," said Haare, when he heard all this. "Maybe we can call the video *Revenge of the Amazon Women*." You can see that Simon has a bad effect on some of his less strong-minded friends.

While he was away, there was quite a lot of arguing in class about whether there could be a part for Simon in the video. All the rest of us were going to be in it, even if it was just in the crowd scenes, but the suffragette business took place about 1900 to 1910, and as someone said, they didn't have electric wheelchairs then.

Becky and Todd and some others reckoned there must be some way we could fit Simon in, even if we just showed him in a head and shoulders shot, or maybe sitting behind a table. But most of the others reckoned it couldn't be done without having to change the whole story. Ms. Kidman stayed out of the discussion, but she was listening hard.

While the others were talking, I was remembering what Mrs. Mason fed into the information chain once about how Simon always missed out on fun when he was a little kid, trying to get along on crutches.

Mrs. Mason said that she'd see other kids coming to play at Simon's, and they'd all muck about there perfectly happily for a while. Then suddenly they'd decide they wanted to play on Dean's swing or on Tasha's slide, and they'd all go tearing off to those places, the way little kids do. All of them except Simon, who couldn't tear off anywhere. Mrs. Mason said he'd just watch them go without saying anything, and then he'd slowly swing himself back inside on his crutches.

And suddenly I heard myself say, "You *can't* leave him out!"

Everyone stared at me. Jason's mouth wasn't the only one hanging open. I felt like a fool, but I knew what I meant. "He's in this class, isn't he? And this is supposed to be a class video. You can't leave him out!"

Most of them still just stared at me, but Nelita and a few others nodded. Ms. Kidman nodded too, and smiled. Then Haare said, "Right on, Nathan," and the others started making *I agree* noises. I was glad I'd said it.

Nelita, who has some quite sensible ideas sometimes, said we could fold rugs over the modern parts of Simon's chair, and he could be a wounded war hero. And I bet he gets fussed over by Brady and the other girls, I thought.

We shot the first scene on Wednesday morning, on the front drive. It was meant to be a big suffragette protest rally in a town where a government official was visiting. Alex Wilson was the bullying, beefy, big-headed official, and Jason was his thick-brained assistant—great character casting by Ms. Kidman.

The girls were the protesters, naturally. They'd all gotten themselves long dresses that reached right down to the ground, and they really looked the part, though Haare, Todd, and I agreed it was a pity to hide Brady's legs. The rest of us guys were a crowd of heckling onlookers—more excellent casting.

Things went pretty smoothly at first. Even Jason didn't forget a single one of his lines. Actually, Jason didn't have any lines. Alex, the government official, arrived and was booed by the suffragettes. The suffragettes were booed by the heckling onlookers. Ms. Kidman said we'd have to do the take again because a couple of fifth formers had wandered past, and she thought they were probably on the video. Ms. Kidman and the fifth formers were booed by everyone.

We were doing our second take when Simon arrived. Us guys acting the heckling onlookers were facing toward the school's front entrance, and I saw the Shaws' van pull up.

Mrs. Shaw, who was driving, obviously saw the suffragettes in action. You couldn't help seeing them. You couldn't help hearing them, either. They were chanting "Votes for us now! Votes for us now!" Us guys were chanting back "Vote for a cow! Vote for a cow!" which made Ms. Kidman look a bit thoughtful at first, but she let us carry on.

Mrs. Shaw stopped the van just by the entrance to the drive. She went round the back and opened the doors. Simon came down on his hoist, and he and his mother watched what was going on. They must have thought the class had gone mental while Simon was in hospital.

Then Mrs. Shaw said something to Simon, got back in the van, and drove away. Simon started whirring along the drive toward the girls, who were blocking the way. I say he started whirring, but you couldn't hear him over the noise of the chanting. The girls couldn't see him, either, because they had their backs to him. Anyway, they were too busy yelling and shaking their fists at Alex and Jason and us. Alex was looking a bit nervous. I think he was hoping they'd remember it was just a video.

Simon came right up behind the back row of girls. I saw his lips moving, so I guess he was asking if he could drive through. They still didn't hear him. I saw him shrug his shoulders—his right shoulder wasn't in a sling any longer—and start turning his wheelchair to drive around the outside of them.

The wheelchair brakes must have jammed, just as they did that other time. Simon's chair started to turn around, then it gave a jerk, turned slightly the other way, and drove gently into the back row of girls.

To be exact, it drove gently into the back of Brady West's knees. I heard her squeak in the middle of the chanting. She tried to jump away from whatever it was that was attacking her, but she couldn't move quickly because of her long skirt.

As the wheelchair kept coming forward, Brady's legs buckled, and she folded gently down into Simon's lap. Without thinking about what she was doing—I hope so, anyway—she threw her arms around Simon's neck for something to hang onto.

The suffragettes in the front row must have sensed something was happening behind them, because they opened up on either side. Simon's wheelchair, carrying Simon and Brady, came straight through them and toward the government official and his assistant. The government official got out of the way smartly. His assistant—it was Jason, after all—stood staring until the wheelchair clipped him across the inside of one knee.

As Simon struggled with the brake control, the chair

rolled smoothly toward Ms. Kidman and the video camera. Simon gave a furious push at his left-hand lever, and the chair halted half a meter away from our English teacher. Brady shot out of Simon's lap as if she'd been stung. Her fair hair had come loose and was tumbling all down her back, and her eyes were enormous. She looked . . . spectacular.

"There you are, lady," said Simon to her. "That'll be a dollar for the taxi fare."

The great thing about making a video, of course, is that you can rewind it and replay it straight away. After Simon's Charge of the Light Brigade, there was nothing else we possibly could do, anyway. The whole class trooped back inside, where Ms. Kidman slipped the cassette into the player.

It was fantastic. Brady hid her face in her hands and wouldn't look. The rest of us whistled and cheered as Simon came trundling out through the ranks of suffragettes—"Like a kamikaze pilot who can't get liftoff," said Haare—with Brady desperately holding on.

"Simon, you certainly know how to sweep a girl off her feet," Ms. Kidman told him.

The best thing of all was that we were able to keep the scene for the final video. Brady's long skirt hid the controls on the wheelchair, and the rest of Brady hid all of Simon except his face, so you couldn't see his school jacket.

"We'll say you're an old soldier from the Crimean War," Ms. Kidman suggested to Simon. "And you've got no patience with this votes-for-women business."

"Do I get another medal for leading this afternoon's attack, then?" Simon wanted to know.

"I was the one who got attacked!" Brady told him.

"Yeah, but I'm the one who was wounded," said Simon. "I mean, I did get squashed."

Todd, Haare, Jason, and I looked backward and forward at one another. I suspect we were thinking that we wouldn't bother about any medals if we had the chance to be squashed by Brady West.

Simon and I are hardly going to see each other during the holidays. I'm going to be down with Dad for the first week. Then in the second week, Simon's off to this Paritai Home for Disabled Children. It's a sort of holiday home where kids can go and give their families a break. Mr. and Mrs. Shaw and Kirsti are having a week in the city on their own.

Simon's pleased they're going to go away. He says that when he first started suffering from muscular dystrophy, Kirsti had to take second place in everything. It was always Simon who had the first shower, Simon who was allowed to choose what TV program they'd have on, Simon who had the bigger birthday party.

Then one weekend, after Simon had been allowed to choose where they were going on Sunday, Mr. Shaw suddenly said, "Hey, this isn't fair to Kirsti."

"No," said Kirsti. "And it isn't fair to Simon, either." She was right, too, Simon reckons. It's good to have to wait your turn sometimes.

Anyway, the Shaws and us role-players are all going to send Simon postcards. So are some of the other kids in the class. "Feelthy postcards, please," he says.

I don't know if Brady is. I let slip very casually to her that I'd be away too, for the first week, but she didn't say anything and she didn't ask for my address. Oh well.

CHAPTER

Eleven

My week with Dad wasn't exactly a great success.

As I suspected, he's got a new girlfriend. Her name's Emma, and she's quite nice. But she was trying to impress Dad, and Dad was trying to impress her, and they were both trying to impress me, and it just didn't feel very natural.

The time I enjoyed most was near the end, when Dad and I spent a day wheelbarrowing a big truckload of firewood into the garage of the place where he's living. We were more relaxed and did some proper talking then.

"Dad, why did you and Mum split up?" I suddenly asked him. I'd been planning to for months, but it still sounded awkward and strange when it came out.

Dad stood there beside the woodpile in the garage, looking

a bit lonely. "It's hard to put into words, son. I'm still very fond of your mother, but . . . well, people can grow apart without understanding it themselves. Perhaps . . ." Then he shut up, stared vaguely at the two bits of wood he had in his hands, wandered outside, and threw them back on the heap in the drive instead of stacking them in the garage.

Grow apart! I'm still trying to think of ways for Brady and me to grow together.

I sent Simon a postcard of the gorilla in the city zoo, with a message asking, "Seen Alex Wilson around town?" And I sent him the latest *Northern Spews* headline—TEENAGE BOMBSHELL'S END-OF-TERM ROMP—with a message asking, "Seen Brady West around town?" I bought Fiona the Moaner a giant eraser in the shape of a dog. Maybe it'll help her remember when it's her turn to take him for a walk.

Dad gave me a present to take home for Fiona, too—a huge white stuffed monkey with eyes that go round and round when you pull a cord in its back. I thought it was absolutely gross, and I made him put it in a plastic rubbish bag before I'd take it on the bus. Fiona squeaked and drooled over it, of course.

Dad also gave me some money for myself, which I didn't put in a plastic rubbish bag, and he gave me a big thick letter for Mum. She didn't say what was in it, but she spent a lot of time in her room over the next couple of days.

Simon went off to the disabled kids' home the day before I arrived back, so the second week of the holidays was pretty boring. Haare was away, too. Mum said he'd rung while I was with Dad, and told her about getting his braces from the orthodontist, except Haare kept calling him an "awful dentist." I had one role-playing session with Todd and Jason. I walked the dog past Brady's place a few times, but I never saw her. I even played cards with Fiona the Moaner and thrashed her.

Simon sent me two postcards. One was a picture of part of the town where Paritai Home was. He'd drawn an arrow pointing to the home, and written a note saying, "My barbed-wire enclosure is here."

The other card showed girls in bikinis on Paritai Beach, and Simon wrote, "Wish you were here." Except he'd put a couple of question marks—"Wish you were here??" His handwriting looked jerky, as if the ballpoint wasn't working properly.

He came home the Sunday before term started, and I went around to his place in the afternoon. It was good to have him back. I said so when Mrs. Shaw opened the door and he came rolling down the hall. "Oh hell, they let you out, then?" I said.

I got a shock when I saw him, though. His neck and face looked thinner, as if he hadn't been eating much. "Didn't they feed you at that place?" I asked before I thought properly. Simon just shrugged his shoulders. "Yeah, but I didn't feel like it."

His chair was different, too. The people at the Paritai Home put a big padded backboard on it. "My neck gets a bit tired now, and I can lean it back against the board," he said. He had a new seat made out of fiberglass, too. It was molded to the shape of his bottom, with a sheepskin rug to pad it. "My bum's getting skinnier," he told me.

"Well, you won't take up so much room around the place, will you?" I said. Simon prefers you to talk tough. He hates anyone getting sloppy and sentimental. But it wasn't easy to say those things this time.

He said the home had been okay. He'd met a couple of kids there whom he'd seen in hospital at different times. The people in charge were happy for him to stay on for another week if he and his parents wanted, but Simon said no thanks, he'd like to be back for the start of term. "The school doesn't run properly if I'm not there to keep an eye on it," he'd told them.

He'd gone out a couple of times for rides in his chair. The home was quite near the beach, but since it was the start of winter, he didn't meet any girls in bikinis. However, he did meet a lot of little kids playing on the sand. They kept asking him things like, was he sick, were his legs sore, why did he have to be in a wheelchair?

The same sort of thing happens sometimes when I'm downtown with him, and he never minds. "Let them ask," he says. "They've got to learn about these sorts of things. I don't mind telling them."

One little kid came up to him outside the dairy once and said, "Are you a spastic or something?" Simon just laughed—you could tell the kid wasn't trying to be cheeky—and said, "I'm a something."

The people he does get angry about are usually the adults

who try to hush their kids up and get them to come away. "That's like pretending I'm not there—pretending I don't exist," Simon says.

Another thing that makes him wild is adults who talk about him as if he's backward or something and can't think for himself. It doesn't happen so much now, but when he was about ten or eleven, people would sometimes say to his parents or Kirsti, "Would Simon like an ice cream?" or "What would he like to drink?"

When this happened, Simon used to butt in. "Just a minute," he'd say, "I'll ask him."

Then he'd start this conversation out loud with himself —"Would you like an ice cream, Simon? Yes, I would. And what flavor, Simon? I'd like strawberry slush. Right, I'll tell them, Simon." He admitted that okay, it was rude, but sometimes you had to educate people the hard way.

After a while, we started talking about Brady. Well, Simon started talking about her—quite suddenly. He looked at me after I'd asked very, *very* casually if he'd seen any kids from school during the first part of the holidays and said, "You'd like to go out with Brady West, wouldn't you?"

You could say that's true. To be really honest, I haven't thought of going out with Brady in the sense of taking her places. Where could I take her with my pathetic pocket money? When I think of *going out* with her, I just have a lot of rather vague but colorful pictures in my mind.

"You'll have to start working out some techniques to impress her," Simon told me. Cheeky sod!

Once again I showed my imperturbable urbanity (look it up!) where the opposite sex is concerned. "Pllrrfggh?" I retorted.

Simon was full of bright ideas. "You could try showing her your muscles and your manly physique," he said. Since my ribs look like the sides of a rowboat and my collarbone's like a coat hanger, I gave him a cool look.

"Or you could try showering her with exotic and expensive gifts," he suggested. Since he already knows about my pocket money, I gave him a cold look.

"Or you could dazzle her with your intellectual brilliance, make fascinating conversation with her on all sorts of absorbing topics," he went on. Since Simon has already heard me say *Fnnffn* and *Rggmhh* to Brady on more than one occasion, I gave him a frosty look.

"Or you can just try being yourself and acting natural," he finished. "If she likes you, she'll show it."

Since the idea of any teenager knowing his real self is ridiculous, and also since this last idea of his was such common sense that it made me feel nervous, I gave him an icy look.

But I was thinking on my way home to do the brontosaurus-walking that it's sad to hear Simon talking about girls. Of course he's keen on them—he's a teenage male. And of course they feel sorry for him and they're nice to him, and they like his sense of humor and the way he's so quick with words. But you realize he's going to miss out on so much. All the things that I worry aren't going to happen to me, he *knows* aren't going to happen to him.

"All this hassle about safe sex," he was grumbl[ing]
way home one afternoon after the class had a talk [with]
Smither the school counselor. "I'd be glad of the cl[ance of]
any sex!"

I felt sort of ashamed. Because Simon's in a whe[elchair]
and because of what's going to happen to him, you [forget]
that he's got physical feelings like everyone else.

I promised myself I'd hang around with Simon [at]
lunchtime at school this term. Sometimes in the first [term]
I'd get bored sitting down all lunch hour, and I'd go [and]
play softball or soccer with the other guys. Simon use[d to]
head off to the computer room when this happened—h[e'd]
never say anything.

When I got home, I even suggested to Fiona the Moane[r]
that she might like to do a drawing for Simon on his firs[t]
day back at school. Mum gave me a surprised smile. Even
the dog lifted his head from where he was snoring and
wheezing on the rug.

The next morning, Fiona gave me a piece of paper showing
someone in a supermarket trolley lining up to check out.

"What's this?" I asked, and of course she started to get
angry. Then I remembered—Simon's First Day Back At
School.

CHAPTER
Twelve

It was an absolutely perfect morning for the first day of term—black clouds down around knee level, wind screaming like Antilla the Hun on an off day, and rain machine-gunning against the windows.

I bullied the brontosaurus out onto the back porch to see if he wanted his morning tree-erosion exercise. He took two steps out into the rain, did a lightning U-turn, and went straight back to his rug.

Meanwhile, Fiona the Moaner was complaining about having to walk a few blocks to school in case her new sneakers got damp. Mum, who's been up and down like an elevator ever since she got that letter from Dad, was having one of her up times this morning and took Fiona in the car. Being the strong silent type, I went on my own feet. I wore Dad's

old parka—it's big enough to squeeze two people into, almost. But there wasn't any sign of Brady.

Mrs. Shaw brought Simon in the van. Their wheels splashed through the front gate at the same time as my feet splashed through, with Simon doing his royal wave from the back window. I waved just a couple of fingers back at him.

By the time I got to the covered walkway, Mrs. Shaw had unloaded Simon and driven off, with a toot, another wave, and another few splashes. I dripped over to where Simon was sitting, all dry and cozy inside his plastic rubbish bag.

Rubbish bag is his name for it. It's a big, clear plastic waterproof apron that he wears in wet weather, otherwise his legs get soaked almost straight away. It comes halfway up his chest, reaches down under his feet, and clips onto his wheelchair.

Simon wears his zip-up school jacket most of the time, even in fairly warm weather. Because he has circulation problems, and because he can't jump and rush about to keep warm, he gets cold easily. And since his chair can't move faster than a medium walking speed, he's liable to get wet if he's caught out in the rain.

He wears long pants all the time, too. Mostly it's for the same reason—to keep warm. But he told me once that he wouldn't wear shorts anyway, because his legs were so skinny and skeletonlike. When he first developed muscular dystrophy, his calf muscles grew big and strong-looking. That happens with a lot of MD kids. But now his calf muscles have shrunk away, too.

"My knees are my widest bits from the hips down," he

said. "When I'm in the shower I'm scared to look at my legs. They're like *The Praying Mantis from Outer Space*."

When we got to our first class, which was metalwork with Mr. Wood—Todd says that at the school he and his stepbrother used to go to, there's a woodwork teacher called Mr. Steele—Simon and I both turned into Jasons. Our mouths fell open at the same time.

Alex Wilson was there, looking embarrassed and sitting in a wheelchair.

It seems he tore the ligaments in his knee during the holidays. He'd been speeding up and down on his BMX outside the house where our local bikers live, giving them cheek. A couple of them pretended they were coming after him, so he jumped on his bike and roared off into the sunset. At least he roared off, but his BMX didn't. It flipped over and sent Alex flying. He ended up with torn ligaments, and one of the bikers ended up taking him to the doctor on the back of his Harley-Davidson. He's going to be in the wheelchair for another week.

Simon thought it was great, of course. He spent the first ten minutes of metalwork doing reverse turns and circles around Alex, saying, "Here, try this one. Here, can you do this?" while Mr. Wood pretended not to notice. And he spent the whole day calling Alex "fellow sufferer" or "comrade" or even "brother."

You had to admit it was a bit of a laugh. I mean, Alex has always been this big macho man who likes showing how strong and massive he is. He goes to weight training and tae kwon do, and all that grunt 'n' groan stuff. Simon reckons he needs some exercises to strengthen him between the ears as well. Mum reckons Alex is secretly afraid of illness and pain. He certainly always seems uneasy when he's around Simon.

He took all the jokes pretty well. He did tell Simon a couple of times to shut up or he'd get smeared over the walls.

"You'll have to stop banging into them first," said Simon.

But mostly Alex just grinned. He even cracked a sort of half joke about challenging Simon to a stock-car race. It wasn't much of a joke for anyone else, but it was pretty fair for Alex.

We didn't do any more work on our video in English. The weather made it hopeless, and anyway, as Ms. Kidman said when she saw Alex, "One of our leading men is temporarily legless."

"I'll be Alex's stand-in, Ms. Kidman," Simon offered. "Or his sit-in, at any rate." The rest of the class groaned. Ms. Kidman refused politely.

So we spent the English lesson making notes and having a discussion about video and television in general—technical words, features to look for when you're analyzing a program, and what makes a good or a bad television program.

Ms. Kidman said she reckoned some television shows were so bad that they'd stopped scraping the bottom of the barrel, and now they were scraping the underside of it. That's good—I'll have to use it in an exam answer sometime.

Then we got on to our favorite TV programs. Haare reckoned you couldn't beat "Play School." Becky Klenner and Lana Patu both said they liked horror movies—just the soundtracks, though. They never actually *saw* them because they kept their hands over their faces. Brady, who had her hair cut during the holidays so that it sort of curves across her cheeks, turned out to like "The Miss Universe Show," which was a bit disappointing. Jason's a fan of hospital soap operas, which is fair enough when you consider how much time he spends in the school sick bay.

My own favorites are wildlife programs, especially on the great apes and suchlike. But since I was sitting just across from Alex Wilson in his wheelchair, I didn't feel it was appropriate to mention this.

"How about your *least* favorite programs?" Ms. Kidman wanted to know.

The arguments started. Everyone agreed that all commercials should be dropped, though Haare kept disagreeing. He said that he thought the one for disposable diapers, where the babies talk in posh English voices, was really choice. Nelita and some other girls reckoned "The Miss Universe Show" was sexist. This made Brady put her nose in the air, which served Nelita right for poking her nose in. Then Simon stuck his hand up.

"Yes, Simon?" asked Ms. Kidman. "Which television shows do you like least?"

"Last year's 'Telethon,' " said Simon straight away.

Ms. Kidman began to nod her head, then she looked puzzled. So did other people in the class. Last year's "Telethon" had raised millions of dollars for disabled children.

"You do mean the 'Telethon,' Simon?" checked Ms. Kidman. "The one for . . . for . . ." It's unusual to see Ms. Kidman not certain of her words.

"For kids like me," Simon finished off for her. "Yeah, that's the one. I thought it was sick."

"Why, Simon?" Lana wanted to know. "It did a lot of good."

"It raised a lot of money, you mean," said Simon. "That's not necessarily the same thing."

"What didn't you like about the 'Telethon,' Simon?" asked Ms. Kidman. "Is it any of the points we've been talking about?"

"Well, I don't think it's good television," Simon began. "I mean, they try to pretend that all the rushing around is unplanned, but you can tell that they've been practicing. And I think the picture it gave of disabled kids was gross."

"Go on," Ms. Kidman said.

"There were two things I really hated," Simon continued. "The first was the way they made it sound as if all people had to do was give some money. Then they could feel they'd done their bit for disabled kids, and go back to their own nice little lives."

As hands started to go up around the class, Ms. Kidman said, "Perhaps we can talk about that later. What was the other thing you hated?"

"It's sort of hard to put into words," Simon said. "But . . . well, how come I'm here?"

"Oh, poor Simon!" called Haare. "Haven't your mummy and daddy told you about the birds and the bees?"

After everyone had finally quieted down, Simon went on. "I mean, why am I at *this* school—an ordinary normal school, except for Haare Haunui?"

"Why not, Simon?" said Nelita. "You should be treated like other kids as much as possible." There were murmurs and nods of agreement around the room.

"Yeah! Right!" Simon agreed. "All the spina bifida kids and MD kids and cerebral palsy kids I know think that, too. They want to live like—live *with*—able-bodied kids as much as they can. That's what my therapy and coming here are all about." More murmurs and nods—nods of understanding, this time.

"So what does the 'Telethon' do? It treats us like outsiders. Makes people feel that as long as they go aaww! and feel sorry for us, we'll be okay. But we won't be. I mean, I know it sounds like something out of 'Days Of Our Lives,' but we don't want your bloody pity, we want your world!"

Haare had a grin from ear tip to ear tip. With his new braces, it looked like the front of a 1938 Ford. Jason's jaw was somewhere down near desk level. Ms. Kidman was smiling and shaking her head.

"Oh, Simon, Simon!" she was saying. "Please write it down. Please put it in your next essay for me."

At lunchtime, I remembered the promise I'd made to myself the night before. While Simon rolled around, I strolled around with him. We went to the computer room and Simon mucked about with a couple of programs. He's pretty good at it. He could have quite a career in computers. Yeah, I do keep forgetting, don't I?

The black, wet, windy morning changed into a blue, dry, windy afternoon. I walked home beside Simon as far as the crossing by the dairy. SMOOTH-TALKING LOVER-BOY LEAVES TRAIL OF BROKEN HEARTS! howled the latest *Northern Spews* poster. "See!" said Simon. "I said you should use the intellectual conversation approach with Brady."

We were looking at the poster when another wheelchair rolled out of the dairy. It was Alex, and Brady was pushing him. They didn't see us as they turned and headed off up the sidewalk. I stared after them and my stomach went heavy.

"Oh, well," said Simon. "Maybe it'll have to be the expensive gifts technique after all, Nathan."

MOUNT PROSPECT PUBLIC LIBRARY

CHAPTER
Thirteen

This Saturday afternoon I survived the ultimate torture. I passed the toughest test of strength and courage. I endured an ordeal that would leave strong men pale and trembling. I did some baby-sitting.

Simon and I did it together, actually. The usual gang was supposed to be role-playing at his place, but Todd was grounded for the weekend after an argument with his step-father, Haare went off to a wedding, and Jason had the mumps. When you look at Jason, you sometimes wonder how human beings have ever managed to rule the planet. If we were all like him, we'd be extinct.

I went round to Simon's partly because there wasn't anything doing at our place. The dog was snoring in front of the fire and giving little yips and yelps in his sleep—Mum reckons he dreams that he's chasing rabbits, but I reckon he dreams that the rabbits are chasing him. Fiona was off with one of her nauseating little mates. Mum said she had some work to do for the afternoon. I've got a feeling she was working on a letter to Dad.

And partly I went because I wanted to ask Simon whether he thought Brady was keen on Alex Wilson. I couldn't believe it myself. How could a girl as cute as Brady like a life-form as primitive as Alex? But I felt I could do with a second opinion.

I didn't get it. When I arrived at Simon's, there was a strange car in the driveway behind the Shaws' van. Mr. Shaw's sister, Simon's Auntie Patrice, had come to visit. She'd brought her new baby—doom!

Kirsti was holding the baby, whose name's Aaron, when Mr. Shaw answered the door. "Isn't he gorgeous, Nathan?" she asked.

"Yeah," I said. No, I thought. He looked like all babies —small and red-faced and dangerous.

"Look, Nathan!" Kirsti exclaimed. "He's smiling at you!"

"Poor kid," said Simon. "He must have something wrong with him."

"It's probably wind," said Mrs. Shaw.

"Waddaya mean, wind?" asked Simon, pretending to look out the window. "The clouds aren't even moving."

"No," said his mother, "I mean wind in his stomach— as you know perfectly well, Simon Shaw. He's not really smiling at Nathan. He's probably going to burp, or maybe sick up a bit."

"Yeah?" replied Simon. "Funny, I often feel that way when I look at Nathan, too. Who's a clever little lad then, Aaron?"

After I'd uttered a few more compulsory coos at the baby, Simon and I escaped into his room to abuse the computer. I was just getting ready to introduce the topic of Brady and Alex—very casually, of course—when Mr. Shaw stuck his head through the door.

"Can you guys keep an eye on Aaron for twenty minutes or so?" he asked. "We're all going down to the shops before they close."

"You mean you're leaving us holding the baby?" said Simon, pretending to be terrified. I didn't have to pretend.

Mr. Shaw laughed. "A couple of cool dudes like you," he said. "You'll be all right."

And for about ten minutes, we were all right. I was just about to have another go at raising the Brady–Alex business when Simon looked up from the computer screen. "Listen!" he said. There was a grizzling, whimpering sound coming from the living room.

Simon rolled through to investigate. I kept a safe distance behind. Aaron was lying in the sort of dog-basket thing babies have for traveling in cars and looking fed up with life.

"What's the matter, mate?" Simon asked. Aaron grizzled louder.

"Maybe he'd like a go on the computer?" I suggested.

"Get real!" Simon snorted. "I suppose you'll be giving him a turn on your ten-speed next!"

I kept my dignity. "D'you reckon he's hungry?" I asked. "I can make him a spaghetti sandwich or something." Aaron grizzled louder still.

"There are times when I wonder how Fiona survived," Simon told the living room. "Pick him up and pass him here."

"With my bare hands?" I asked. But I lifted Aaron out of his dog basket and put him in Simon's lap.

Simon was incredible. He held Aaron against him while he drove his wheelchair around the living room and up and down the hall. After a few laps, the grizzling changed to grunting. After a few more, the grunting changed to snoring—*norsing*, as Fiona used to call it.

"You've got to have the touch," Simon said. "Okay, back to the computer."

Simon kept Aaron on his lap while we carried on programming the computer with names of people we'd like to donate to medical science. You can see how I was hoping to bring up Alex Wilson's name. The baby slept on. After a while, he turned sideways and burrowed his face into Simon's sweater to get more comfortable. Simon grinned down at him. "Disgusting little vermin," he said.

He looked so good with Aaron, I couldn't help thinking how tough it is that he's never going to have any kids of his own. It's a bit the same with his parents—after Simon's muscular dystrophy was diagnosed, the Shaws knew that if they had another son, he had a fifty percent chance of getting the disease, too. So Mr. Shaw had that operation to prevent him from having any more kids. A vasectomy, I think you call it?

Aaron was still fast asleep when his mother and the Shaws came back from the shops. "Sshh!" hissed Simon as they came down the hall. "You'll wake him up!"

Aaron's mother, Simon's Auntie Patrice, shook her head in pretend amazement. "If I hadn't seen it, I wouldn't have believed it," she said.

"I have seen it," exclaimed Kirsti. "And I still don't believe it. Did you guys bore him to sleep or something?"

"Jealousy," said Simon. "Some people can't recognize natural talent."

Mrs. Shaw was standing behind the others. She looked at Simon with his little cousin asleep in his lap, and her eyes flooded with tears. She turned away before Simon could see her and went back down the hallway. I remembered Ms. Kidman at the back-to-school dance.

When I left to go home, Kirsti said she had to go to the dairy so she'd walk part of the way with me. Her parents are the sort of shoppers who always forget at least one vital thing, she reckons.

I didn't object. As I've said before, it does your reputation no harm at all if you're noticed in the company of a seventh-form girl. It's clear that mature females find you attractive.

Almost as soon as we got outside, Kirsti started talking about Simon. "Mum and Dad and Auntie Patrice reckon he looked just like Aaron when he was little," she started off.

Poor Simon. I'd have to tell him that the next time his head started getting a bit too big for his headrest.

"When he was about six or seven, and they were starting to realize he had MD, he suddenly asked Mum if he couldn't be a baby and start all over again. Except this time, could he please be made like other kids? Mum howled her eyes out."

Kirsti's own voice was a bit shaky itself. I didn't know what was the best thing to say to her, so I said what I felt, "It doesn't seem fair."

Kirsti nodded slowly. "And when he was about a year older than that, he came home one morning from Sunday school all excited. They'd been telling him about praying, and how everyone's supposed to have a special line to God. He couldn't wait to get to bed that night and start saying his prayers. He thought all he had to do was ask God once, and when he woke up in the morning, his legs would be better."

This time I didn't know what to say or think, so I kept my mouth shut. We walked on together for a few seconds, before Kirsti spoke again.

"Do you know Rachel Tennant at school?"

I looked vague. I've never found it hard.

"The fifth former who belongs to that very religious family?" Kirsti said. A couple of low-wattage bulbs came on inside my skull. I nodded.

"She asked Simon once if he'd tried praying. And you know what Simon's like. He said they must have a pretty useless request program in heaven, because nobody had gotten back to him."

I laughed. I could imagine Simon coming up with a line like that. Kirsti laughed too.

"Then Rachel said to him, 'Well, didn't it make you feel better, anyway? Don't you feel easier after you've told someone your problems?' Simon said his mouth slid open so far he expected her to start calling him Jason. He realized she was dead right."

I nodded again. I nodded wisely this time. Hadn't I been trying to make myself feel better all afternoon by telling someone about Brady and Alex Wilson? Without any luck, mind you.

"Typical Simon, though. He can't let anyone else have the last word. He told Rachel since it was also supposed to make you feel good when someone told you their troubles, he was glad he'd helped keep them feeling useful up there."

I said what I thought once again. "He's quite a guy."

Kirsti agreed, "He is, isn't he?"

We reached the dairy. Kirsti looked at me just before she went inside, gave me a smile that I wished half our class had been passing by to see, and said, "You're a neat kid, Nathan."

As I continued on along the sidewalk, there was a gray cat crouching beside a fence, watching me. I remembered Mum saying exactly the same thing. "You're a neat kid, Nathan." What is this mysterious attraction I have for older women? I could do without the *kid* business, though.

Then I stopped, and said something that made the cat vanish under the fence. I'd missed the chance to sound Kirsti out on her opinion of a possible Brady–Alex relationship.

CHAPTER
Fourteen

As it happens, I needn't have bothered. A lot of things have happened in the last week and four-sevenths.

Mum checks the letter box at least five times every afternoon when she comes back from work. She's expecting something, and I reckon I can guess what it is. I notice she hasn't been getting any lifts with Mr. O'Rourke lately.

Other newsworthy events have included Mrs. Kuklinski hitting the dog with a lump of dirt after it washed out a new rosebush on her front lawn, and the dog spending the next two days hiding inside. The *Northern Spews* came out with a headline—TERRIFIED GIRL WATCHES AGHAST. I showed it to Simon and he said, "That's strange, I haven't seen any ghasts around for a while." Something else has happened with Simon which I'll get to in a minute. And Brady West isn't speaking to Alex Wilson!

Alex has been out of his wheelchair for over a week now. Maybe Brady has a thing about men in chairs, after having Simon scoop her up during the suffragette video, but I saw Alex limping along the corridor on the way to social studies, saying something to her, and she was completely ignoring him, just walking on with her nose in the air. She can make you feel about half a centimeter tall when she does that. You could tell that Alex didn't have a clue what to do. I almost thought *poor old Alex*, but I won't go that far.

I still haven't managed to bump into Brady again in the mornings. But I have met up with Nelita a few times. She's quite good to walk with, really, though she does keep on with these sick jokes—"Doctor, Doctor, I've just swallowed a ballpoint!" "Well, sit down and write out your name."

And she is a bit inclined to try and run other people's lives sometimes. Simon's shirt had come out the other day —it often does when he moves around in his chair. He has to wear shirts with tails or else his back gets cold.

He was having trouble getting his shirt tucked in again, since he can't reach back behind him, so Nelita said, "I'll do it, Simon." Next thing you know, she's fussing round him, pushing the tail of his shirt back in.

There was no reason why one of us shouldn't have done it, of course, and Simon didn't seem to mind at all. Then Haare calls out, "Nelita, what *are* you doing to that young man? Keep your hands to yourself."

"Shut your face, tin teeth!" said Nelita. Haare, who's still a bit sensitive about his braces, didn't say anything more. Simon thought it was hilarious.

Simon is getting worse quickly now. He had to go back into hospital suddenly this week. It was just for one night, not even long enough for Fiona the Moaner to do him a drawing—lucky escape, Simon.

Mrs. Shaw rang up and told Mum. Simon had started finding it hard to breathe properly after tea on Wednesday, and Dr. Mehta told the Shaws to take him straight to hospital. By the time he got there, he was okay again, but the hospital kept him overnight for observation.

I know from what he's told me that this is another thing muscular dystrophy does. The muscles around your chest and shoulders get weaker, and it's harder for your lungs to work properly.

Simon's deteriorating in other ways, too. He can't be bothered to do his physical therapy exercises in phys ed, like he's supposed to do, and he's not interested in doing anything at lunchtime. When I ask if he wants to go to the computer room or the library, or maybe just drive around a bit in the corridors, he shrugs his shoulders and says, "Up to you." It makes me annoyed, even though I try not to let it.

When Mum passed on the phone message from Mrs. Shaw, she looked at me for a second and said, "How do you feel about Simon, love? How do you think he is?"

I was wandering around the living room, and I just shook

my head. Then, since Mum was still there, and still waiting for an answer, I made myself say it. "I think he's going to die pretty soon."

Things were very quiet after I'd spoken. I could hear Fiona and the brontosaurus playing out on the back lawn, and I wondered for a moment if they might succeed in exterminating each other. I should be so lucky.

I wasn't looking at Mum, but I could feel her nod. Then she said, "Nathan love, it's all right to feel frightened. And to feel angry."

It was such an amazing, mind-reading thing for her to say that I turned into a Jason for a few seconds.

"You're upset about him. And you're upset about yourself, too. That's only natural."

I sent out a couple of toll calls to my bottom jaw, and hauled it back up into a more or less normal position.

"You always feel angry when you lose someone who's important to you. Your Dad and I . . ." Mum went silent for a moment, then started again. "Anyway, look at Mrs. Kuklinski—when her husband died, she was so angry and upset that she cut up his photo with her nail scissors!"

I couldn't help laughing at the idea, and suddenly I found I still had a voice. "Did she really? I never knew that."

"Yes," said Mum. "And she said it took her nearly all the next morning to find the bits of photo in the wastepaper basket and tape them back together."

Outside on the back lawn, Fiona was holding up a bit of biscuit. The dog was trying to haul its stomach off the ground and reach for it. Never mind the biscuit, I tried to tell the stupid animal by telepathy, eat the thing that's holding it.

"I do feel angry," I told Mum. "I mean, he's such a really neat guy, and he could have such a great life." I remembered what I'd said to Kirsti on the way to the dairy. "It doesn't seem fair. Not when it happens to someone his age."

"I know," said Mum. "Once upon a time, kids and old people were the ones who did the dying. Now it's just supposed to be the old people."

"I mean, it's different if it's an accident." I was working out what I meant as I said it. "Todd Martin's stepsister, remember? She got killed when that car knocked her off her bike. And I know there's no cure for muscular dystrophy and all that. But you just don't think about kids Simon's age dying of disease. Not in this country, anyway."

The dog had eaten the biscuit. Now it was laundering Fiona with its tongue, searching for any crumbs. I sent off another telepathic message, reading "Slobber her to death."

"It's the wrong order of things, isn't it?" agreed Mum. "A kid dying before his parents. Poor Mr. and Mrs. Shaw. They're having to handle something that doesn't have any rhyme or reason to it."

"It's not fair," I heard myself saying again. Maybe I was turning into a parrot.

Mum put her hand on my shoulder. She used to reach down to do that, but over the past few months, it's been more of a reaching straight out. See what comes of eating all your veggies?

"Like I said, love, it's only natural to feel angry." On the lawn, Fiona was aiming a kick at the dog.

"But don't let it take you over completely. You can put too much of your life into feeling angry. It damages you after a while." The dog was now hiding behind the clothesline. Fiona was trying to kick it with both feet at once.

I knew Mum wasn't just talking about me and Simon—she meant something else that was pretty close and private to her. So I told her something private in return.

"I'm not frightened about Simon. It's going to happen. Nobody believes they'll suddenly find a miracle cure or anything like that. I know I'll miss him, but there's nothing I can do. And that sort of makes it easier. There's one thing that does get me sometimes, though."

Fiona managed to half land a half kick that wouldn't have bruised a sand fly. The dog yelped and howled and rolled on its back. Its stomach wobbled like jelly in a fur coat. Fiona dropped on her knees beside it and started hugging and smooching it. Maybe she'll catch rabies or typhoid.

"Yes, love?" Mum was waiting for me to go on.

"Well, sometimes I feel guilty—Simon being crippled while I'm fit and healthy. But . . ."

"That's perfectly natu—," Mum started to say.

"Hang on!" I interrupted her. I was just getting warmed up. So was the dog—it was licking Fiona's face. The typhoid chances were rising.

"But even though I feel guilty, I feel glad, too. Glad that I'm okay and there's nothing wrong with me." It was just as well my little sister was on the other side of the window—I'm not sure she'd agree with the last part.

"That's right," said Mum straight away. "And you're excited almost, because the world feels somehow special, bright and shiny and full of good things that could happen."

It's always a shock when you find out that your parents are intelligent after all. I looked at Mum and she nodded. "It's true, isn't it, love? You can feel both glad and sad at the same time. You know what I mean?"

I stared through the window at Mrs. Kuklinski's trees, bending and bowing against the white winter sky, and I felt an excitement about—oh, about life and the future rise up inside me. Yeah, I knew what she meant.

Fiona and the brontodog were sitting side by side on the lawn. The bront was exhausted from three minutes' exercise and was heaving and panting with its tongue hanging out. Fiona was heaving and panting too, though so far she'd managed to keep control of her tongue.

Just then she looked up and waved. Waved at me, mind you. As I've said before, the brat has no respect for her betters.

Normally I'd have done what I usually do and pretended she didn't exist. But I was feeling so good after talking to Mum that before I could get a grip of myself I grinned and waved back.

Mum smiled out at Fiona and then smiled at me. "She can be a dear little thing sometimes, can't she?"

I don't believe in perjury, so I didn't say anything. Anyway, looking at Fiona and the dogosaurus had reminded me—I must cut out that other *Northern Spews* headline and take it along to Simon when he comes back tomorrow. It said: ALIEN BEINGS IN OUR MIDST?

CHAPTER
Fifteen

Today I walked to school with Brady! I walked to school with Brady today!

Simon rang me up this morning to tell me his mum was taking him to school in the van, so I'd have to find my way down the road, round the corner, past the dairy, and along the sidewalk all by myself. Cheeky little . . . person. His mother wanted him to stay home for the day, but he'd told her it was the school cross-country race, and he wanted to be there to count the death toll. I've been trying to forget about the race.

I'd been thinking I might see Nelita on the way to school. I'd even found a joke that I thought would be just her level—"What's black and white and red all over?" "A newspaper?" "No, a zebra with diaper rash."

But I did better than seeing Nelita, I met Brady!

She must have been wearing some perfume or something, because she smelled really fantastic, just like a department store. She must have guessed that I was feeling a bit uptight about Simon, because she didn't say anything about him— she just talked about last night's television programs. I managed a few *nggrrftt*s, and I think I nodded in a pretty cool sort of manner. She didn't say anything about Alex Wilson, either. Tough luck, Alex!

Simon was waiting in the social studies room when we arrived. He didn't look too bad. He was talking to Nelita and Haare and complaining about the cold.

"It'd freeze the feathers off a brass duck," he told me. "Don't you reckon?"

"Yeah," I agreed, though I didn't really think it was all that bad. I could see Simon was wearing an extra jersey under his school jacket.

"I think I'm getting a cold," said Haare hopefully. "My annual cross-country cold."

The day of the cross-country race is the time when half the kids at school try to make out they've got colds or the flu or yellow fever or something. Unless they've got a note from their parents, Mr. Johnston just laughs and tells them that fresh air and exercise will do their lungs good. All phys ed teachers are sadists.

But then there are those who actually look forward to the race. Brady West is one of them. I heard Lana Patu telling Becky Klenner once that it's because Brady likes showing off her legs, and Lana had noticed Brady always seemed to have a new pair of shorts for every cross-country race. Just jealousy, I reckon. Anyway, Brady's legs aren't her only gorgeous feature.

Alex Wilson is another cross-country nut. After that business a few weeks back with his knee ligaments, he had a perfect excuse not to run, but the thought never seems to have crossed his mind. I mentioned this to Simon, who said it probably couldn't find anything to cross. You have to admit that Alex is keen on sports.

It was Jason whom we were feeling most worried about. Jason is a guy who can choke on a lunchtime sandwich, poke himself in the eye as he tries to reach over and slap his own back, and then sprain the wrist of his slapping hand. Sending him out on a cross-country course with ditches, fences, creeks, and steep hillsides seemed a bit like telling someone to go out and play on the motorway. Haare, Todd, and I decided to run with him. We wouldn't look so bad that way.

We spent a fairly depressed morning in class, trying to make ourselves look pale, and trying out a few hollow coughs. As we ate lunch, Simon advised us, "Eat up, warm up, run up, throw up." He was getting all perky at the thought of the suffering he was going to watch. We changed into our sports gear and started wandering out to the cross-country starting line.

It's a sort of tradition at our school that you can wear almost anything you like to run the cross-country race.

Maybe it's a let-the-condemned-victim-have-a-last-treat idea. Maybe it's so they can identify the corpses more easily afterward.

So I was wearing a T-shirt with a picture of the Mona Lisa smoking a cigar—Dad gave it to me last year. Haare had on an old gray tracksuit top with *Return to Sender* written on it in red felt. And Todd had a T-shirt with a stencil that said *If you can read this, you're smart enough to be a teacher*.

Lana and Becky must have got theirs from the same shop. Lana's read *Math Rules: 0 + K?* while Becky's said *Politeness Rules: If you don't mind*. Jason had an army shirt with *Blood Group A* in big letters across one pocket. Maybe he thought it was a good idea to have that information close at hand.

The teachers had already headed off to their various checkpoints. They're supposed to stand at different places around the course and make sure you go in the right direction. Otherwise half the school might disappear into the swamps and not come back till the exams are over. It would make a good *Northern Spews* headline—CRAZED TEENAGERS RUN AMOK. Except, as Simon would no doubt point out, *Northern Spews* readers probably don't know what a mok is.

It nearly did happen last year, in spite of the teachers. Well, because of the teachers, actually. Ms. Kidman was supposed to be looking after one particularly important place on the course where kids had to turn left. If they turned right, they were liable to end up running sideways through the kids heading for another checkpoint. That might lead to alarm, confusion, and the odd punch-up.

The trouble was that Ms. Kidman took a book out on the

course with her. She wanted to have something to read while she was waiting for the runners to arrive.

Now Ms. Kidman is a cool teacher, but she gets a bit hot and bothered if someone interrupts her while she's rapt in a book.

This must have been a particularly interesting book, because when the kids started puffing and panting up to her, Ms. Kidman stared at them vaguely and waved her hands in all directions. Kirsti Shaw, who's quite a good runner and who'd been leading the senior girls till then, came in fourteenth for the intermediate boys. A couple of third-form girls who'd been about eighty-sixth and eighty-seventh when they got to Ms. Kidman suddenly found they were out in front of all the senior boys, and ran faster than they ever had in their nasty little lives.

So this year Ms. Kidman was writing down names at the finish line. Mr. Packman was with her. Since he's a science teacher, he can probably calculate the chances of anyone surviving the run.

The most important checkpoint on the course was being controlled by—aaarghh!—Antilla the Hun. No way was anyone going to turn the wrong way this year. When Antilla says, "Jump!" all you say is, "How high, sir?"

Simon was trundling along with us. He was going to watch from the top of a bank just beside the finish. He said he'd play "Dixie" on his wheelchair horn every two minutes. It would be like a rescue beacon if Jason got lost. He could aim toward it.

To be exact, Simon wasn't trundling. He was being trundled. His wheelchair batteries were both being recharged, and he was having to get people to push him.

Pushing Simon in his chair is not on my list of Fun Things for Weekends. As I believe I've mentioned, his chair is *heavy!*

Even getting it up onto the sidewalk where there's no ramp is a major project. Tip chair back, taking weight on rear wheels. Lift front wheels onto curb by pushing rear wheels forward while passenger grips armrests and shuts eyes. Lift back of chair up, heaving and panting, while front wheels threaten to roll back and passenger starts shouting lots of advice. Push whole chair forward and hope rear wheels make contact on sidewalk surface without jolting passenger forward onto face. Measure damage to heart and back muscles while passenger says grateful things like, "Whaddaya doin'? Trying to put me into orbit?"

So when we saw the bank that Simon wanted to watch the race from, there were groans and moans from the four of us.

"What are ya? Men or mice?" Simon jeered as we stopped at the bottom.

"Squeak! Squeak!" we all replied.

Haare and Todd got behind the chair. I went in front to hold the footrests and pull. "I'll put my feet on Nathan," said helpful Simon. "That'll make it easier."

There was a bit of discussion over where Jason should go. We didn't want him near any sharp parts of the chair in case he got stabbed, or near any heavy parts in case he got crushed. Finally we agreed he should go behind Haare and Todd and push them.

We lined up at the bottom of the bank. "Forward, my faithful servants," Simon ordered.

I pulled. Todd and Haare pushed. Jason pushed Todd and Haare. Next thing you know, there's a shriek from Haare, and he's lying on the ground twitching and writhing. A broken back? A severed nerve in the leg? No—Haare's ticklish, and Jason accidentally pushed him in one of his sensitive bits.

We regrouped, with Jason pushing Todd only. We heaved. We hauled. The chair stayed put. Three turd formers passing by started to get smart, then scattered as Todd took a couple of steps toward them.

We tried again. The chair struggled up the damp grassy bank about two meters, then slowly slid back down again. "I could grow old right here," said Simon. Brady West came past in a pair of glossy blue running shorts and matching top. She looked at us in a nonadmiring way. Hell!

"Maybe if you four get in the chair and I do the pushing?" suggested Simon. We ignored him and strained with all our strength. The chair skidded round in a half circle and ended up facing away from the bank.

There was a noise behind us like corrugated iron sliding down a pile of bricks, and I recognized Alex Wilson's laugh. "You guys want to put more sugar on your cereal!" he sneered. "Let a real man have a go!"

The real man waved the rest of us aside and got in behind the chair. He held the back supports with both hands and lunged forward. Movement! No, not the chair—Alex. His feet slipped backward about half a meter. Jason and Haare stared thoughtfully at the ground. Todd stared thoughtfully at the sky. I stared thoughtfully ahead of me.

My stare met Simon's eyes. One of them slowly closed and opened in a wink, then flickered downward toward the controls of his wheelchair.

My own eyes moved in the same direction, and I produced a snort which I quickly changed to a cough. Simon had both wheelchair brakes on! No wonder we hadn't been able to move the little fink! No wonder Alex was still floundering like a seal trying to push a tugboat.

I moved back to the wheelchair. "I wonder if we might try it a different way," I said in my most polite voice and gave Simon a meaningful look. He winked his other eye, and I saw his hands move on the controls.

To my surprise, Alex seemed almost grateful. I suppose I'd saved him from looking stupid by himself. And I suppose Mum's right—Alex is sort of imprisoned by his own macho image.

Anyhow, we both grabbed the chair's back supports, bent our backs, and pushed. This time, the chair rolled smoothly forward and up the bank. In fact it almost raced up the bank. Alex obviously has more muscles than the ones in his head. I was struggling to keep up.

There were cheers from the others, and I heard Nelita yell, "Great stuff, Nathan!"

We bounced up to the top of the bank and stopped. "Thanks, guys," said Simon. "Consider yourselves hired."

Alex let go of the chair, gave me a vast grin, and thumped me on the shoulder, stopping the blood flow to one arm. It's his way of saying thank you. I let go of the chair with my undamaged arm, briefly considered a return thump, but decided against it.

Then, as we opened our mouths at the same time to say something pleasant to each other, the wheelchair gave a lurch. There was a gasp from Simon, yells from behind us, and suddenly the chair was over the lip of the bank and rushing down the other side. On the damp grass, Simon's brakes had failed to hold the wheels.

Alex snatched at the chair and just missed. Simon was carried bucking and bouncing down the slope. I could see his hands clinging to the armrests. Somehow the wheelchair stayed upright and straight till it reached the bottom of the bank. Then one of the wheels jolted against something, and it slewed round and capsized. Simon fell onto the grass.

Alex and I were down beside him so fast that the wheelchair still hadn't finished toppling over. Alex grabbed it before it could land anywhere near Simon. "Oh, hell, mate!" he was babbling. "Jeez, mate, are you all right?"

What I did was completely wrong, of course. Every first-aid book tells you that you shouldn't move or even touch accident victims until you're sure they haven't got any broken bones. I came swooping in like some mad mother duck and scooped Simon up in my arms.

It was like picking up someone made of plywood and paper. He seemed hardly any heavier than a basket of dry washing when you carry it in from the line. His useless legs flopped and the top part of his body fell sideways against me. His shoulders and arms were shaking, and his face was white and trembling. There was a grass smear across one shoulder and down his arm where he'd fallen, but otherwise he didn't seem to be hurt.

As Haare and Todd and the others came tearing up and over the bank, Simon's eyes jerked. He seemed to realize what was happening and how I had a hold of him. "Oh, Nathan!" he said. "This is so sudden! What will Brady think?"

Then he looked over my shoulder to where other anxious faces were appearing, and he called out, "Ms. Kidman! Mr. Packman! Please tell this person to put me down. I don't know where he's been!"

There was general chaos for the next five minutes. Simon was checked, and his wheelchair was checked, and they both seemed to be all right. Nelita arrived with two blankets from the sick bay. Simon was lifted back into his chair, and the blankets were tucked around him. He was glad to have them—he was still white and shaking, though of course he was trying like hell to hide it.

"Ah'm okay, pardner. Jest leave me here with m'gun and m'dog," he said, which had a few people looking baffled. And when he saw Jason, he called out, "Now that's what you call a *real* accident!"

Someone went and got Kirsti. "Running your own cross-country, were you?" she asked Simon when she came. Then to me, "Thanks, Nathan." I didn't deserve it, but I felt like Mr. Universe.

Kirsti and a couple of other seventh formers began wheeling Simon back to the school. "I'll ring up Mum and ask

126

her to come," said Kirsti. "I think this BMX maniac should be at home for the rest of the day."

Unfortunately, everyone else remembered then that a cross-country race was supposed to be happening. Haare suggested to Mr. Johnston that the event could be postponed for a year or two. "We sensitive types are feeling a bit shaken, Mr. J.," he said.

Simon was just being moved off when he heard this. "They need the exercise, Mr. Johnston!" he called back. "Especially Alex and Nathan—they can't even catch an invalid in a wheelchair!"

CHAPTER
Sixteen

You know those times when things don't seem to make sense?

I don't mean things like math which has never made sense to me. I mean things in general. The last week has been like that. Nothing's gone the way you'd expect it to.

For a start, Simon wasn't even hurt after trying to do his own cross-country race. We all thought he'd be in hospital for sure, but no. He stayed at home for a couple of days, then he was back at school again. He even got us to come and have our usual Saturday afternoon role-playing at his place. "We're going to try this Galactic Flight game," he told Haare, Todd, and me. "Didn't you notice how expertly I flew through the air the other day?"

But if Simon didn't end up in hospital, someone else did. You guessed it—Jason.

After Kirsti had taken Simon off, the sadistic teachers made the rest of us run the cross-country course after all.

But some of us—Jason in particular—only ran part of it. He, Haare, Todd, and I came wheezing and gasping up to the checkpoint where Antilla the Hun was standing. Antilla glared at us and snapped, "Fourth-form boys? That way!" We groaned on past.

Then Jason, who has the memory span of a backward amoeba, turned round as he was running and started bleating, "Mr. Antill? Mr. Antill, did you mean go round the trees or straight through the—" *Thunk!* Jason had made his own mind up. He'd gone straight through the trunk of one of them. He spent the night in hospital with a mild concussion.

For the first few hours he was there, he kept grabbing passing nurses and saying, "Where's the finish line? Where's the finish?" Simon said it was a pretty clever technique to use on females. But we all agreed that since Jason's love life has hardly even begun, it's rather early for him to be worrying about the finish.

Life at home hasn't been making much sense, either. There was a letter for Mum a few days ago, and I recognized Dad's handwriting. Since then she's been away with the fairies. She's either sending Fiona the Moaner and me out of the room while she talks on the telephone, after which she comes out blowing her nose and wiping her eyes, or else she's going out for half-hour walks by herself. She even forgot to get dinner one evening, till the dog started whimpering and chewing on the table leg.

Then, while she was out on one of her walks, I had to deal with another crisis.

Fiona and one of her septic small friends were playing in her room, and they got into an argument. Don't ask me what about—one of them probably pulled a Barbie doll's head off without anesthetic or something.

When Fiona and her friends have an argument, the script always reads the same—"Did so!" "Did not!" "Did so!" "Did not!" You start to feel like you're at a Ping-Pong tournament.

This time it ended with doors slamming and the friend tearing off down the path, yelling that Fiona was mean and she didn't *ever* want to play with her *ever* again, *ever*. I was nodding my head in agreement when my small sister came blubbering into the living room, chucked herself onto the sofa beside me, and started howling all down the front of my new T-shirt. Dad sent this one, too—*Make love, not war: Apply within*. He's got taste.

I'm not paid to do this sort of thing, but I put one arm around the brat's shoulders and patted her for a moment. It's a technique I learned with the dog. Then I suggested she might like to do a drawing for Simon. After all, it's been a while since he's really suffered.

She went scuttling off to her room, and in about ten minutes she'd produced another Fiona original. It was pretty impressive, really. It showed a fighter pilot being catapulted out of his aircraft's ejector seat over some mountains. The ejector seat was still spinning through the air, and troops were firing at him from way down below.

"Not bad at all," I told her. "Where's his plane?"

Fiona stared the way only little sisters can stare. "What plane? It's Simon falling out of his chair at the cross-country race, like you told Mum about. There are all the other high school students pointing at him."

She gave up in disgust and went off to play with the dog. The dog's life has been confused, too, lately. For one thing, Mrs. Kuklinski has had a new, wire-mesh front fence put up, and the dog can't get to one of his favorite erosion areas. For another, he's finding out that no matter how long he stands with his nose pressed up against a spiderweb, the spider refuses to come and jump into his mouth. All that happens is that he gets a double nostril-load of sticky threads, and goes around sneezing on the carpet for the rest of the day.

Like everyone, I sometimes think how life would be so much simpler if you were an animal. There would be no relationships to get upset about, no meaning of life to find out. Then I look at the dog and decide to stay as I am after all.

Even at school things have been weird. Alex Wilson actually gave me a nod as we went into metalwork the morning after the cross-country race. I think it was a nod, anyway. It may just have been his brain going rollabout again. It's not all that easy to tell with Alex.

Our class has been different, too. Usually, even in a fairly easygoing class like ours, there are a few kids who get treated differently from the others. Someone's a victim—maybe just for a couple of days, or maybe, for the unlucky ones, the whole time they're in school. People start giving Nelita a hard time because her jokes are getting on their nerves. The girls reckon Brady West is so fond of herself she should wear a mirror in front of her face. Kids imitate the way Jason's mouth hangs open. Even Alex Wilson gets sarcastic remarks made about him, usually when he can't hear those remarks.

The last few weeks haven't been like that. Nobody's actually said so, but I reckon that as Simon's been getting weaker, the rest of the class have been getting kinder to one another. Maybe they feel that since they can't do all the things they'd like to do for him, they'll do them for each other. Or maybe it's like I said to Mum—when you look at Simon, you feel lucky and guilty, and that makes you want to be kinder to others. Kind—aren't these four-letter words disgusting?

Ms. Kidman seems to have noticed it, too. The day after Simon's cross-country air-male attempt, she suddenly told us all at the end of English, "I've always enjoyed teaching you lot as a class, and I want to say how this term has made me admire you as people. You're growing up to be an impressive lot of human beings—even if you still can't spell properly."

Of course, we reacted the way impressive human beings always do when they have flattering things said about them.

We shuffled our feet and went pink, and we tripped one another up and punched one another on the arm as we were going out of the room. And we felt good.

But I'm just getting to the really strange part of the week.

I think I've made it clear that walking to school for a while now has been a bit like flipping a coin. Sometimes the coin lands face up, and Nelita walks with me. The latest Nelita joke is "What's green and white and goes *boing-boing*? A spring onion." Sometimes the coin lands face down, and I walk by myself, feeling like I've fallen on my own face. A very few times the coin seems to land on its edge, and Brady comes down the sidewalk at the same time as I do.

The coin's been face down more than usual this term. That's partly because Simon comes to school in the van all the time now. With his breathing problems getting worse, Mr. and Mrs. Shaw don't want him out in the cold for long. "I'm sort of a precious hothouse flower," Simon told us at role-playing. "Probably a Venus' flytrap."

But for most of the last week, I've been walking to school with *two* girls. Brady seems to be leaving home at the same time as me, and Nelita has been coming out of her street at the same time as we go past. It's either that, or I've finally found the right aftershave, which is not very likely since I've only ever shaved twice.

The funny bit is, though Brady almost seems to be making a point of walking with me, she never has much to say—just a few things about television programs, where their family is going next holidays, and their new car. Mr. West's new car has a personalized license plate that says, ALL MYN. I have my doubts about Mr. West.

Most of the time though, Brady just walks beside me, or beside Nelita and me, looking around as if she's expecting someone. It's Nelita who does all the talking. She always asks about Simon, and she's always got something to say about school and the teachers.

She does most of her talking to me. She's always polite to Brady, but I don't think you could really call them friends. A couple of times she's said something to Brady, and when Brady obviously hasn't been listening, Nelita's rolled her eyes at me. I try not to grin. Anyway, Brady is pretty fantastic even when she's just walking.

Then today, after this had been going on for a week, the three of us were just arriving at school when Alex Wilson came round the corner of the building.

He looked a bit embarrassed at first. Then he mumbled, "Hi, Brady."

Brady had been looking around the way she usually does. The moment Alex spoke, she snubbed him dead. She turned to Nelita and me, butted straight into what we were saying, and started talking and laughing as if it was party time. Then the moment we'd left Alex behind, she stopped talking and walked off without taking any notice of us.

Nelita rolled her eyes at me again. She's got quite nice green eyes, as it happens.

Then we both stared back at Alex. Alex threw his arms out wide, almost bowling over a couple of passing third formers, gave a gi-normous shrug, went down on his knees, and pretended to be praying. Then he and Nelita and I all burst out laughing.

As I say, it hasn't exactly been a week where things make sense. The latest *Northern Spews* headline gasps: RADIO STATION STAFF ORDERED NOT TO TALK.

CHAPTER
Seventeen

I guess that in the last few days, things have started making sense again. Too much sense, in the case of Simon.

He'd been off school on Tuesday afternoon, seeing Dr. Mehta, and he rang me that night.

"Got something really weird to show you tomorrow," he said, knowing this would annoy me.

I retaliated by asking one of my probing questions. "What?"

"Patience is a virtue," said Simon. "And I bet you can't spell either of those words." But he didn't sound very happy about things.

As soon as I got to school next morning—just Nelita today, no Brady—I saw why. Simon's got a strap across his chest, holding him in the wheelchair.

It's been getting harder and harder for him to sit up straight as his back muscles weaken, and when he slumps down in the chair he starts to have problems breathing properly. The strap is a broad elastic belt that goes across his chest and under his armpits. He can loosen or tighten it to make himself more comfortable. Rather, he can ask someone else to loosen or tighten it for him. He isn't comfortable very often now, and his family is still having to turn him in bed at night.

I suppose there's nothing else the doctor could do, but the strap looked bloody awful. It reminded me of the illustrations we saw in social studies last year of little kids in mines about a hundred years ago, crawling along narrow tunnels and pulling a coal wagon behind them with a rope tied around their bodies. It made me angry to look at it.

Simon felt the same, I'm sure. He tried to joke about it, snarling and making his hands into claws and going, "Keep back! Savage DoberSimon!" But you could see the expression in his eyes.

I knew the sort of thing he'd want me to say. "Hey, they finally realized you're a mental case! They finally put you in a straitjacket!" I joked.

"Fair enough, eh?" said Simon, and he relaxed a bit.

Everyone else was pretty shocked by the strap, too. Mostly they didn't know what to say. Some of them tried to act as if there was nothing different about him. That annoyed Simon, of course. He can't stand it when people won't face what's happening. He rolled his chair up close to a couple of them and said, "Hey, would you like a belt? I'll give you a belt!" I've said it before, he doesn't make things easy for people.

Some kids were good. Jason said, "Sorry you're all tied up just now," which is probably the wittiest thing Jason's ever said in his whole life. Maybe he's still feeling the effects of the concussion.

Haare said, "Hey, you're lucky they didn't use wire, like they did on my braces!" Todd made out Simon had nicked the belt from his trousers and he was worried about his pants falling down.

Lana and Becky and Nelita all came across at the start of science and asked, "Hi, Simon. Anything you want?" Simon said, "Yeah, but it might get me expelled." They giggled, and Nelita pretended to pull his ears.

I asked him at lunchtime if he wanted to go to the computer room, but he said, "Nah, I'm feeling beat, actually." So the usual five of us just sat around in the classroom and talked about girls, and role-playing, and girls, and the cross-country race. And girls.

Later, in math, where we were all sitting like little pixies with our hands folded while Antilla the Hun growled about some problem, I heard a quiet wheezing sound. Simon had dropped off to sleep in his chair. Antilla noticed him, but he didn't say anything. The Age of Miracles must be starting!

Mrs. Shaw gave me a lift home in the van with Simon after school. After all, it's winter and I'm a fairly delicate hothouse flower myself.

I didn't hang around long. You could see that Simon was

still tired. I helped Mr. Shaw for a few minutes while he moved the footrests on the wheelchair. Simon's supposed to sit with his thighs parallel to the ground if possible—it keeps his back straighter and helps his breathing. But now Mr. Shaw's moving the footrests up to see if that'll sort of push Simon's backside up against the back of the chair and help keep him upright.

"Check the garden for me, will you, Nathan?" asked Simon as I was leaving. "It's probably time I got out there with the rotary hoe."

Mr. and Mrs. Shaw had made Simon a garden of his own three or four years back. It's an old bath that they got from a secondhand shop. They put the bath up on some railroad ties at the bottom of the ramp to the back door and filled it with soil. It's just the right height for Simon to reach from his chair. He grows carrots and lettuces in the bath, though he reckons he's planning to switch to marijuana. He says that's the real cash crop these days.

Things are still a circus at home. Every afternoon when Mum comes home from work, she wants to know if there are any letters for her. Every time the phone rings, she knocks over three chairs as she sprints to answer. It's one of Fiona's mates nearly every time, of course. I reckon they should just graft a cellular phone onto my sister's ear—it'd make things simpler for everyone.

The dog's given up on spiders, and now he's into hypnotizing birds. He spends most of his time crouching under the flowering cherry tree on our front lawn—since it's on our lawn, he's not interested in irrigating it—and staring up at the starlings and fantails. Maybe he hopes they'll laugh so much at him that they'll get giddy and fall down.

Nothing much else has happened at school. Simon was away on Thursday—he told me over the phone that he hadn't woken up till half past ten that morning. His mother had let him sleep. "She said it'd mean a few less breakfast dishes to wash." He looks tired nearly all the time now.

Just as well he was away, probably. Instead of social studies, we had a talk from Mr. de Witt, the careers advisor. I don't need to tell you that everyone calls him Mr. Half-Wit. He was asking us what plans we had for our lives ahead, and I could just imagine the sort of thing Simon might have said. It made me think of that discussion we had with Ms. Kidman in English about getting old, way back in the last term.

There were some quite amazing career ideas from the class. Jason wants to go into medicine—he already is, half the time! Brady wants to be a flight attendant—hmmmmm. Nelita wants to work with little kids. Haare says he's going to be a male model, and Todd says he's planning a career in chicken farming. What am I going to be? I haven't a clue. Unemployed, probably. But it's always interesting, talking about your future.

On Friday, just after tea, the phone rang. Mum knocked over a small table, upset a vase of flowers, sent the dog under the sofa, grabbed the receiver, and said, "Oh hi,

Simon. No, of course he's not doing anything useful. Hang on, I'll let him off his leash."

"No role-playing tomorrow, sorry," Simon told me, after I'd worked my way across the wreckage of the room and gotten to the phone.

"Why not?" I asked. Yet another probing question.

"I've got to go back into hospital. Dr. Mehta says she's fed up with me sounding like a leaky plastic bag when I breathe. She wants to try me on a new lot of antibiotics, and she wants to be there while I take them. I'm thinking of hiring myself out as a guinea pig."

"What time are you going in?" I asked.

"Tomorrow morning. Want to come round and check that I'm not smuggling Brady West in with me?"

"Who?" I asked.

Simon laughed, started to cough and gasp, said, "Aaarghh! The Black Death!" and hung up. I hung up, too, and stared at nothing much. Mum looked at me for a while, but didn't say anything.

In some ways, the next morning at the Shaws' place was like it was that other time Simon went into hospital. He was cleaning up his bedroom and grumbling because he didn't think it was untidy. There were two bags packed— the small one with dressing gown and pajamas, and the big one with role-playing gear.

Kirsti was telling Simon to make sure he took his washcloth. "He says he can't stick his arm out properly and reach the faucet in the sink now. You grubby little boys are all the same." Kirsti's hair was just washed, the same as it was that last time, and I still couldn't think of anything cool to say to her about it.

But today some things were different. It isn't just that Simon is so thin and tired-looking, it's the way his parents look at him.

"They're having to handle something that hasn't any rhyme or reason to it," Mum had said, and I could see what she meant. Mr. and Mrs. Shaw kept watching Simon, especially when they thought he wasn't noticing. A couple of times Mrs. Shaw seemed as if she was going to say something, but she didn't. It's hard to put it into words, but I felt the whole family was *ready* for something, and they all knew this without having to say it out loud.

I wasn't going to the hospital with them this time. They hadn't asked me, and you could tell they wanted to be by themselves. While Mr. and Mrs. Shaw were carrying things out to the van, and Kirsti was in her room using the hair dryer, Simon and I were left by ourselves.

We didn't say anything for a minute or so, then Simon said, "Reckon you lot can manage at school without me for a few days?"

"Aw yeah," I said. I'm always at my most eloquent at these moments.

"That other muscular dystrophy guy I told you about," Simon went on. "Sione—he used to reckon it was hardly worthwhile our going to school because we'd never get the chance to use what we learned. That's bullshit. I'm glad

I've gone. Anyway, I've got to keep an eye on you and Brady, eh?"

"Aw yeah," I said again. I was right—I *am* turning into a parrot.

"Mind you, I reckon you're working on the wrong girl there."

I was just going to ask him what the hell he meant by that when Kirsti and Mrs. Shaw came into the room.

"Ready, Simon?" asked Mrs. Shaw.

"Ready, *mein Führer,*" said Simon. "Hey, I wonder if it's fish and chips and fresh fruit salad again tonight?"

Then he stuck his hand out to me. I was a bit startled. I don't think we've ever shaken hands before. It looked kind of weird, too. Simon was only able to put his hand out from the elbow down. It felt dry and warm.

"No worries," he said. "It's nothing to do with me now. See ya, Nathan."

"See ya, Simon."

Mrs. Mason had come out into her front garden to see the Shaws off. Simon did his royal wave to us both till the van disappeared around the corner.

The streets on the way home seemed strange. I suppose it was because I was wrapped up in what I was thinking, but it felt as if the shrubs and even the houses were listening to me going past. Pathetic, I know, but everything was so quiet.

It wasn't quiet when I got home, though. My first thought when I opened the back door was that we'd won the lottery or something. Mum was sitting at the table with a great shiny smile that started at one ear, lit up her eyes, turned up her mouth, and traveled straight on to her other ear. Fiona the Moaner was skipping and squeaking around the room as if someone had lit a fuse under her—good scheme that, I must keep it in mind. Even the dog was waving a paw in the air in a confused sort of manner.

Fiona squealed it out before Mum could even get her mouth open. "Daddy's coming back! Daddy's coming back!"

Believe it or not, the first thing I did was to stare around the room, as if Dad might be perched up on the ceiling somewhere. Then I felt my own face turning itself into a huge loopy grin. I looked at Mum.

Mum nodded. She was still smiling. "No promises, Nathan, love. No promises. But your Dad and I have been doing a lot of writing and talking and sorting out, and we both want to try things again. Just to see if it'll work."

"Fair enough," I said, keeping Fiona at arm's length. The insolent life-form was trying to jump up and hug me. "After all, it worked for quite a long while before, didn't it?"

"That's right," Mum managed to get out, just before she disappeared under a heap of leaping, gibbering eight-year-old. "That's right, it did."

That was Saturday. Now it's Sunday and I still keep grinning when I think of Dad coming home. It'll be neat to get told off by *two* parents again.

I was going to go to the hospital this afternoon, but Mr. Shaw rang up to say that Simon hadn't had a very good night, and could I wait till tomorrow? They'd put him on a respirator a couple of times to help his breathing, and he was much more comfortable now.

Fiona's doing a drawing for me to take to Simon, and she's doing another drawing to give to Dad when he comes home next Saturday. Poor guy, he doesn't know what he's stepping back into. A couple of Fiona's drawings and he could end up in the same ward as Simon.

CHAPTER

Eighteen

School on Monday was a depressingly familiar business.

I should have been warned when I saw the *Northern Spews* headline—CHILDREN TELL OF CLASSROOM SUFFERING. But it wasn't till Antilla the Hun handed me back my math test, marked 7/20—*Sloppy work. See me*, and also gave me Simon's, 6½/20—*Hold the calculator the other way up next time*, that I realized the *Northern Spews* must have reporters everywhere.

I walked home by myself that afternoon. No Nelita. No Brady. No Simon, of course. I was planning to go and see him after tea.

When I saw Mum's car in the garage, I was a bit surprised. She doesn't usually get home from work till half an hour after me. She picks up Fiona from a grisly mate's place on the way, so I usually have half an hour's free time with the television and the biscuit packets.

Mum was standing in the middle of the dining room when I came in the door. "Hi, Mum," I said, original as always.

"Hello, dear," Mum replied. Then she took a breath and said, "Nathan, love, I'm sorry."

I knew straight away. I felt I could almost have said the next words for her.

"Mr. Shaw rang me at work just after lunch, love. Simon died at about half past ten this morning."

My face felt thick and heavy. There was a sort of thudding noise in my head. I didn't say anything, just nodded.

Mum went on, "Mr. Shaw said he died in his sleep. It was very sudden and very peaceful. He just stopped breathing."

I nodded again. I knew I had to say something.

"I beat him on the math test," I mumbled.

Mum looked worried. "Are you all right, love?"

"Yeah, Mum. I'm all right. Thanks for telling me."

It was a quiet, quiet evening. Fiona the Moaner didn't come home till after tea. Mum must have told her, because she didn't say anything, just stared at me a few times till Mum bustled her off to bed early.

I took the dog for a walk. Mum offered to do it, but I said I wanted to. He didn't water blast even a single shrub. Maybe he's turning over a new leaf. Maybe he's turning over a whole tree full of new leaves.

Then when I got home, Mum made me sit down on the sofa. She sat down beside me and put her arms around me and I howled for a bit. There, I've admitted it. I felt a lot better afterward.

Oh yeah, one other really weird thing happened that evening. At about nine o'clock, the phone rang. Mum answered it, looked surprised, then said, "Yes, he's here. I'll just get him." She put her hand over the mouthpiece and said, "It's Alex Wilson."

Alex Wilson? I thought. Hell, what have I done? I haven't been talking to Brady.

"Hello?" I said, ready to spring away from the phone if necessary.

"Oh, yeah. Hi, Nathan, it's Alex here."

"Hi, Alex," I said cautiously.

"Look, mate. I've just gotten back from tae kwon do. Todd was there and he told me about Simon. Just wanted to say I'm sorry, eh? You've been a really good mate to him. See you tomorrow, eh?"

"Thanks, Alex." I hung up and shook my head in wonder. You never can tell.

Mum took another phone call from Mr. Shaw the next morning, just as we were finishing breakfast.

"Nathan, Mr. Shaw says that Simon . . . Simon's body will be at home this afternoon and tomorrow morning. He was wondering if you wanted to go there after school. Any of the others can go too, of course."

"Yeah, Mum. All right."

"You don't have to go if you don't want to, love."

"No, Mum. It'll be all right."

Just before I left for school, Fiona gave me a drawing. "It's for you. It's you and Simon." Okay, that choked me up again. Mum gave me a hug. So did the brat, before I could fend her off. Still, I can always wash my hands at school.

Everyone at school knew about Simon. News goes round like a television bulletin in our small town. All the teachers—Ms. Kidman, Mr. Packman, Mr. Rata, Mr. Johnston—told me how sorry they were. Even Antilla the Hun said to me, "My sympathies, Nathan, my sympathies," and praised me for having nearly gotten an answer right.

The other kids were really good, too, even if a lot of them weren't sure what to say. I felt sort of special. Then I felt ashamed of feeling that way, though I guess it was perfectly natural.

Haare, Todd, Jason, and I didn't know what to do with ourselves at lunchtime. We wandered over to the computer room, then to the library, then we just mucked about outside. I think we all half expected to hear Simon's chair come whirring round the corner any moment, with him making some smart crack about how we looked like sheep waiting for a ride to the butcher's.

There's one other thing that I suppose I'd better mention.

Todd, Jason, Haare, and I decided we'd go round to the Shaws' straight after school. A lot of the other kids were going there later—even Alex, though you could tell he was scared. I think Nelita talked a fair few of the girls into it. She told them Mr. and Mrs. Shaw would appreciate their coming.

But when I asked Brady if she was going, she just stared at me and said, "Uggh, no! I think it's a horrible idea, going to look at someone's dead body. What would anybody want to do that for?"

At first I felt so angry that I wanted to yell at her. Then I felt enormously sorry for her. I just turned and walked away. I'm not blaming her for not wanting to come. Like Mum said, it's not something you have to do. But I think I'm clearer about a few things now.

Anyway, there were teachers and kids from other classes as well, all planning to visit the Shaws and say good-bye to Simon. It could be quite a party!

We four role-players were the first to get there. Mrs. Shaw answered the door, and you could see straight away she was really pleased we'd come. Her face was all blotchy, but otherwise she looked all right.

She said that Mr. Shaw had gone out for a walk by himself for a little while, but he'd be pleased to know we'd come. I gave her Fiona's drawing, which I'd decided to bring along. She looked at it, said, "Oh, Nathan!" and went away into her bedroom for a few minutes.

Kirsti was there, too. She kissed each of us on the cheek. I think Jason tried to sneak round to the back of the line and get another turn. She put her arms around me and squeezed me really tight. I can tell you now that girls are constructed quite differently from guys! Then she took us into the living room, where Simon's body was lying in its coffin.

They'd put the coffin across four dining room chairs, and they'd moved the living room furniture back against the walls. There were lots of flowers on the chairs, and on the floor to one side. They'd even put some of Simon's favorite role-playing games on a small table at the foot of the coffin, which I reckon was a neat idea.

I don't think any of us quite knew what to do at first. Then Kirsti said, "Come and see him," and we all went forward together.

Simon was wearing his best corduroys and sweater, and the zip-up leather slippers that he'd started using to keep his feet warm. He looked long—tall, I suppose I should say. It made me realize that I'd never seen him standing and straight.

His hands were together across his chest and his eyes were closed, but there was a tiny glint of the left one showing. I wouldn't have been all that surprised if he'd suddenly winked at me.

I'd had this silly idea that he might already have changed color, that he would be starting to turn green or something. But he looked exactly like he usually did, just a bit pale. You could smell soap—I suppose they'd washed him in the hospital.

We all looked at him for a while. Haare was murmuring quietly in Maori, and I think the rest of us were all saying something inside our heads.

Then, one after the other, we all touched him once on his forehead. It was cold and smooth. I started to choke up again, but I said, "Cheers, Simon," and turned away.

In the hallway, Mrs. Shaw hugged us—I reckon I've equaled my usual yearly tally of bodily contact in one day —and we left. The others had their bikes, but I wanted to walk home by myself.

The afternoon seemed all clean and clear. Every little mossy crack and tire mark on the sidewalk stood out. I knew I'd done the right thing in going to see Simon, and I wasn't angry at Brady anymore.

I felt sort of lifted up. It was like that time I was talking to Mum about Simon dying, and she'd said that the world was bright and shining and full of good things that could happen.

I remembered how I'd looked out the window at Mrs. Kuklinski's trees bending and tossing under that white winter sky and been grabbed by the feeling of how good life was in spite of everything. And I remembered the time, after Simon read his poem in English, when every bit of jealousy and bitchiness I'd ever had just vanished completely. It'd be great if you could keep on like that forever.

Simon's funeral is tomorrow afternoon. Nearly all our classmates are going, though a couple of them say they're not sure if their parents will let them. Poor silly parents, I reckon. Nelita asked if she could come with me, because she's feeling a bit nervous, and I said sure. Now there's someone who'll enjoy headlines from the *Northern Spews!*

I'm not expecting any big changes. For example, I know

I'll never be real friends with Alex, but I'm going to try and be fair about him. Give him a chance, sort of. The same with Brady. I made a mistake about both of them.

I'm not expecting any miracles with Mum and Dad, either. Dad comes home on Saturday. That'll be great. I guess he and Mum are giving each other some more chances, too, and admitting that they made mistakes. We'll all have to see what works out. Life goes on, eh?

Mine goes on without Simon, but with all sorts of memories of him. He was bad-tempered and funny. He was fierce-tongued and brave. He was my friend. I'm proud I knew him, and I'll never forget him.

See ya, Simon.

ABOUT THE AUTHOR

David Hill is the author of several plays and short stories for children that have been published in New Zealand and the United States. This is his first novel for young adults. He lives in New Zealand.